For Sascha and Dani—soulmates;

and for Peppy, unfazed by river crossings.

Chapter One

"Jessa. What a way to spend your birthday!"

Jessa Richardson sat on the edge of the bathtub beside her mother. Her legs quivered.

"I hate throwing up."

"I know, sweetheart. Here. Wipe your face."

Jessa took the cool face cloth and pressed it to her forehead. Having the flu was bad enough. Having to cancel her twelfth birthday party was a disaster.

"Do you feel a bit better? Why don't you crawl back into my bed and watch a bit of TV."

Without argument, Jessa slowly made her way across the hall to her mother's room. Just the thought of climbing the stairs all the way to her own bed in the attic made her feel weak.

Jessa pulled the covers over her head and closed her eyes. The television set droned in the background, a cushion of noise lulling her to sleep. She didn't even notice when her dog, Romeo, crawled up onto the bed beside her.

"Jessa? Jessa, are you awake?"

Romeo's muffled grumble from under the covers eased her into consciousness.

"I have some exciting news for you."

Warily, Jessa poked her head out from under the

blanket. Her mother stood in the doorway of the bedroom holding a mug.

"I brought you some broth."

"That's the exciting news?"

"No, you noodle. The broth is a bonus birthday present. I just had a call from your Granny Richardson."

Jessa sat up slowly. The edges of the room were soft and blurry. "Is it dark already?"

"Almost. You slept all afternoon."

"What did Granny say?"

"Happy birthday, of course. And, she wanted to tell you about your birthday present."

Jessa had been a little surprised when the mailman had failed to bring anything from her grandmother. It would have been rude to say anything, as if she only wanted to get mail from Granny if the package contained a gift. Usually, Granny Richardson sent a parcel the week before her birthday and then Jessa had to wait patiently until May 2 arrived before she was allowed to open it. It drove her crazy having to wait.

Her Omi, her mother's mother, lived in Germany. She always sent a card with some money so Jessa could go shopping and choose a gift for herself.

"Have some broth and I'll tell you what Granny said."

Jessa took the mug and had a small sip. It was the first food she had eaten in two days. The flu had started a week earlier with a cough. After two days of that she'd run a fever and developed a splitting headache. When the headache subsided a bit, the nausea had started. Jessa was sick and tired of being sick and tired.

"How would you like to go on a trip?"

"What kind of trip?" There was nothing Jessa wanted less than to have to go anywhere. At least, nowhere farther than the bathroom across the hall. She reached under the covers and patted Romeo on the head. For a change, Jessa's mother didn't say anything about him being in the bed instead of on the floor where she felt dogs belonged.

"Guess."

"Japan?"

Jessa's father lived in Tokyo with his new wife and baby and Jessa had every intention of visiting them someday.

"Not quite so far away."

So, it wasn't a trip to Japan. Where, then?

"Vancouver?" Sometimes Granny Richardson invited Jessa to come and spend a weekend in Vancouver. Then they would go to the Science Centre, Stanley Park, and Chinatown.

"Farther away than that. I'll give you a hint. This present involves your favourite animal."

Jessa was mystified. "Horses?"

Her mother nodded and gestured to the mug. Dutifully, Jessa took another sip. She swallowed and tried to ignore the queasiness in her stomach.

A trip that involved horses, not to Japan but farther away than Vancouver? "Do I get to go to horse camp again?"

"Nope."

"I have no idea." Jessa stared into the hot, yellow liquid in the soup mug but couldn't bring herself to drink any more.

"How about a week-long trail ride in the Rocky Mountains?"

"Really?" Jessa handed the still-full mug back to her mother and lay back against the pillow. She closed her eyes and sighed. If only she were well enough to feel excited.

"You are booked to leave on the twenty-eighth of June, the day after school ends."

"Can I take Rebel?"

"No. Sorry. Flannigan's, that's the trail-riding outfit, has their own horses. Besides, it's a bit far away to trailer him. You'll be flying to Calgary and then someone from Flannigan's will pick you up at the airport and drive you to the lodge where guests stay the first night. It's near Lake Louise."

Jessa couldn't imagine starting her holidays without her bay pony.

"But who will ride Rebel when I'm away?"

"Jessa, don't be difficult. This is a wonderful opportunity for you to—"

Jessa interrupted. "I know! Maybe I can get Cheryl to exercise Rebel for me while I'm away."

Jessa's mother sat awkwardly on the side of the bed. She patted Jessa's leg.

"That probably won't be necessary."

"What do you mean?"

"I didn't want to upset you, but since you haven't been out to the barn all week and you've been so sick, Mrs. Bailey called to ask if it would be okay for Molly Becker to exercise Rebel. Just until you feel better."

Jessa struggled to sit up again, ignoring the pounding in her head. "Molly who?"

"Becker. That's Sharon Davies' granddaughter."

Sharon Davies kept her horse, Billy Jack, at Dark Creek Stables. Jessa didn't see her too often because Sharon Davies usually rode during the day when Jessa was at school.

"A complete stranger is riding Rebel? And you said that was okay?"

"Hold on a minute. Molly isn't a complete stranger. Mrs. Bailey and I discussed it and thought it was better for Rebel to be exercised—"

"But, Mom! I don't even know this kid! How old is she?"

"Eight."

"Eight? She's not old enough to ride alone!"

"Who said anything about her riding alone? Mrs. Bailey is supervising her. Nothing is going to happen to your pony. Try to be sensible."

Jessa swung her legs over the side of the bed.

"Where are you going, young lady?"

"To the barn."

Even as she said it, Jessa knew she wasn't going anywhere near Dark Creek Stables. She'd be lucky to get across the hall on time.

"Ohhh," she groaned. "I'm going to be sick again!"

Chapter Two

"When are you coming back to school?" Cheryl asked on the phone.

"Tomorrow, I think. It's a good sign that I'm sooooo hungry! I can't remember the last time I felt this hungry!"

"Maybe you still have germs. Just don't breathe on me, okay? I don't want to miss as much school as you."

"Two weeks," Jessa concurred. It had been so long she was actually looking forward to seeing everyone again.

"Are you scared about flying to Alberta by yourself?"

"No," Jessa lied. "The airline will assign me a flight attendant to make sure everything's okay."

"Like a bodyguard? That's so exciting! You can pretend to be a movie star!"

"I don't think so." Pretending to be a movie star was more Cheryl's style.

"How will you get from the airport to the lodge?"

"The trail guide will pick me up at the airport."

"What if the guy's a kidnapper?"

"Dressed like a cowboy and carrying a sign saying 'Flannigan's'? Yeah, right."

"It could happen."

"Only in the movies."

"Do you get riding lessons? So you know how to steer Western style? Will there be other kids?"

"Cheryl! Enough questions! No, I'll be the only kid,

and it can't be that hard to ride Western. Maybe Walter Walters could show me how before I leave. It doesn't matter, though—the brochure says 'instruction is provided—no experience necessary.'"

The last part of "necessary" was lost when Jessa choked back a coughing fit.

"You still sound pretty sick."

"I'm almost better," Jessa insisted, covering the receiver as she coughed again. "It would have been worse if I'd been sick and had to miss the trip."

"Yeah, who cares about missing school. Cancelling the trail ride would have been tragic!"

"No kidding! Hey, do you know a kid called Molly Becker?"

Cheryl cleared her throat on the other end of the line. "Um, not personally. But I heard a rumour she was riding Rebel. Rachel told me."

"Rachel? How would she know?"

"Who knows how Rachel knows the things she knows?"

Jessa's stomach growled. "Well, she won't be riding him for long. I'm going to the barn tomorrow after school, no matter what."

"I just remembered something else Rachel said."

Jessa fought the impulse to hang up the phone. She had a creepy feeling she didn't want to know what else Rachel had to say.

"Well, Jeremy and Rachel were on this trail ride—"

"She was riding with Jeremy?!" Jeremy's mother, Rebecca Digsby, was one of the country's top trainers and worked for Rachel Blumen's father on his estate. Jessa didn't know that Rachel and Jeremy had started riding together. Jeremy didn't even like Rachel!

"That's not the point," Cheryl went on. "Near the golf course, on the beach trail, they saw Molly on Rebel riding with Sharon Davies on Billy Jack."

"Are you sure it was Rebel? It could have been another bay pony. . . ."

"Truthfully, I thought Rachel was kidding. But then Jeremy came over to our table at lunch and asked if you had stopped riding Rebel."

"What! Wait until I get back to school. I'll straighten out all these stupid rumours. Of course I'm still riding Rebel. Why wouldn't I be? Molly was just riding him temporarily until I got better. And now I'm better so Molly will just have to find herself another horse." Jessa muffled another cough.

"I wouldn't be so sure of that."

"What do you mean?"

"Rachel said Molly wants to take Rebel in the pony hunter class at the next Arbutus Lane show which, I believe, is happening on July 1."

"She can't do that! Rebel is my pony!"

"How are you going to stop her? You're going to be off in the Rocky Mountains somewhere."

"Look, this is obviously all some kind of big misunderstanding. Nobody else is going to ride *my* pony in any shows and that's final! Rachel doesn't know what she's talking about! I'm going to the barn after school tomorrow—and I'll tell Molly exactly what I think."

"Jessa, honey. Maybe you shouldn't ride today anyway. You still aren't back to full strength."

"I'm fine!" Jessa ignored her mother and stared in fury at the small figure who was riding around the ring at Dark Creek Stables. Mrs. Bailey stood in the middle of the ring and shouted instructions.

"Don't let him run on like that! Circle, circle—soften your hands—that's it! Good, Molly!"

"Jessa, please don't be so angry. Don't you see it's best

for Rebel to be exercised? Mrs. Bailey couldn't do it herself. . . ."

"And a downward transition to walk . . . very good! Give him a pat and let Rebel have a loose rein for a minute."

Mrs. Bailey pushed her black cowboy hat firmly onto her head. "Hello there, Jessa. Good to see you back on your feet! How are you feeling?"

"Fine."

"That doesn't sound very 'fine' to me! Molly has been doing a great job of keeping Rebel in shape, don't you think?"

Jessa glared across the ring at the small girl who was sitting astride Rebel.

"I've been talking to Molly's mother about possibly letting Molly ride Rebel a couple of times a week. What do you think?"

Mrs. Bailey ignored Jessa's stony silence.

"It seems to me that it won't be long before you need to find a bigger horse to ride, one who can handle larger jumps. We were lucky to find someone like Molly who is such a good match for Rebel now that you're ready to move on."

Move on to another horse? Jessa shook her head slowly but didn't trust herself to speak. *Mrs. Bailey was out of her mind! Didn't she understand that it wasn't that easy for Jessa's mother to just "find another horse?"*

Money was always tight at the Richardson house. That's why Jessa had to work at Dark Creek Stables several days a week to help pay for Rebel's board. *Besides,* Jessa thought, *Rebel was a great pony and so far, there was nothing he couldn't do. His flat-work was excellent, and she jumped boldly and neatly. How could Mrs. Bailey have failed to notice all of that?*

"For now, you'll be fine on Rebel. But really, this summer you should think about moving up, even part-time."

"But Rebel . . ."

The corner of Mrs. Bailey's mouth twitched into a crooked smile. "Rebel's not going anywhere even if you're not his main rider. I talked to his owner. Rosa's just as pleased to have him stay here indefinitely."

"You talked to Rosa?"

Jessa couldn't conceal the quiver in her voice. She could hardly believe that Mrs. Bailey had taken it upon herself to contact Rosa Panini to discuss the terms of Jessa's free lease. Shocked, Jessa turned to her mother. She was horrified to see her mother was nodding, as if she knew all about the changes that were in the works.

"Don't I have any say in this at all?" Gravel crunched under her boots as Jessa turned and stormed back to the car. She slammed the door and slumped into the seat, her arms folded across her chest. She refused to look at her mother when, a few minutes later, she settled into the driver's seat.

"Jessa, please. Be reasonable. Nobody said you have to stop riding Rebel immediately. Just that you might want to start thinking about moving up. Mrs. Bailey says you have the talent and ambition to go a long way with your riding. But Rebel is getting on, you know. His knees are not what they used to be. You're getting taller by the minute and he's not going to grow with you."

Jessa clenched her teeth and stared out the window. As they pulled out of the driveway, she watched Rebel cantering around the ring, his ears pricked forward and his long, black tail streaming out behind him. She closed her eyes and willed herself not to cry.

"I'm riding him tomorrow and I don't want that girl anywhere near me."

Jessa knew she sounded spiteful but she didn't care. Nobody could force her to give up Rebel. They were wrong. He was totally devoted to her and Jessa would prove to everyone that she would not betray the trust she shared with her pony.

Beside her, Jessa's mother drew in her breath as if to say something but then seemed to think better of it. Jessa figured she was getting off easy with a stern glare. If she hadn't been sick so recently, no doubt she would have been banished to her room for the rest of the weekend.

Chapter Three

"I can't wait for school to finish," Jessa groaned. There were only a few days of school left, but they seemed to be lasting forever.

Cheryl laughed and nudged Billy Jack so he came up alongside Rebel on the trail. Recently, Cheryl had been riding the old horse to help keep him in shape because Sharon Davies had very little time to ride. Even though Billy Jack was quite a bit bigger than Rebel, he was lazy. It was an effort for him to keep up with Rebel's brisk walk. "You say that every year, starting in September!"

"That's not true!"

"Yes it is, Miss If-only-I-could-go-to-horse-school-I'd-be-perfectly-happy."

There was no question where Jessa would rather spend her time: the barn, the barn, or the barn. Still, this year had been different. The timing of her flu couldn't have been worse.

There weren't that many hard and fast rules at the Richardson house, but "No riding until your homework is done" was one of them.

"I thought we were going to have to cancel our ride today because of your science experiment."

"Pumpkin seeds!" Jessa said. "I could have failed Grade Six because of pumpkin seeds!"

"All seeds need water. That's pretty basic."

"Like I don't know that. I was busy trying to think of

an ending to my stupid short story about ancient Egypt. I didn't have time for those dumb seeds."

"How much time does it take to give your plants a drink? Besides, the story was an easy assignment."

Jessa clucked to Rebel and he started to trot. She didn't feel like talking any more. The whole point of being out on a trail ride was to forget about the stresses of school.

Cheryl might have had a point that by June Jessa was always itching to spend more time at the barn. But what Cheryl didn't know was something Jessa hardly wanted to admit to herself. It wasn't just the extra school work that had kept her from riding recently—it was exhaustion. Each evening after supper Jessa had to fight to stay awake. Her recent need for an early bedtime was not something she wanted to share with Cheryl, who was the kind of person who came alive after dark.

Jessa wasn't herself during the day, either. It seemed she had lost a lot of fluids during her bout of flu, because she couldn't keep away from the water fountain at school—and that meant that she couldn't keep away from the bathroom, either. It was getting more than a little annoying to barely be able to get through a single class without having to make a trip to the girls' room.

"Jessa! Slow down!" The more Cheryl urged her old horse forward, the more his ears flopped backwards. "You know old Billy Jack here can't keep up with Speedy. Give us a break. So, when are you going to have your party?"

Jessa shrugged. Sometimes, Cheryl had a knack for asking irritating questions. Her birthday party was something else she needed to fit in—but when?

"I have an idea."

"What?" Whenever Cheryl said she had an idea, Jessa

cringed. Her friend's ideas were often more trouble than they were worth.

"Don't be so grumpy or I won't tell you."

The horses passed over the low bridge over Dark Creek, their hooves drumming a hollow pattern on the heavy timbers. Jessa heard the crabbiness in her voice and softened her tone.

"Fine. What's your idea?"

"We could have a joint party in August!"

Cheryl's summer parties were always theatrical productions involving costumes and games and sometimes even performers. Jessa remembered one year's barbecue when a young man in black and purple tights juggled blazing clubs while standing waist deep in Cheryl's hot tub.

"What kind of party will you be having?"

"I haven't decided yet. But we could easily do something together. What do you think?"

"I'll get the gate," Jessa said, hopping off Rebel. She led him into the field behind the barns at Dark Creek Stables. She wasn't going to admit it, but what she was thinking was how badly she needed to go to the bathroom. Aloud, Jessa said, "Having our parties together would be fun."

"Great! We can start planning the minute you get back from your trip. Come on, Billy Jack. Get moving!"

Cheryl hauled on Billy Jack's reins and pulled his head up out of a thick clump of grass by the gate post.

"Jessa, could you give me a hand moving the last of the hay bales up in the loft before you go? I'd ask Walter but his back isn't so good any more."

Mrs. Bailey was old, but she was tough and strong. Jessa followed her up the ladder from the tack room. Moving hay wasn't exactly her favourite job. Even though school was finally finished, Jessa was still catching up at the barn. There were lots of jobs to do on top of her regular chores.

"I've got more hay coming on the weekend. We should move the bales that are left over to the side—make sure you use these up first when you're feeding."

Jessa nodded, struggling to shift the first of the heavy bales. "We'll do them together. Save my back . . ." Mrs. Bailey grunted and they pulled the bale forward together.

"You've been so quiet lately. Cat got your tongue?"

Jessa shrugged. She wiggled her fingers under the two taut lines of binder twine, waited for Mrs. Bailey's nod, and heaved. Forgiving Mrs. Bailey wasn't easy. There was no excuse for her to have made plans about Jessa's riding without any consultation.

"Are these heavier than the last ones we moved?" It seemed to Jessa that it was harder than usual to lift the hay.

A pair of piercing blue eyes looked her up and down from under the brim of Mrs. Bailey's cowboy hat. "Personally, I think that flu took more out of you than you'd care to admit. Back in the old days, bed rest, fluids, and more bed rest were the cure. I think you tried to get back on your feet too soon."

Jessa sighed. She hadn't wanted a whole lecture, just confirmation that the bales seemed heavier.

"Sit down and rest a minute, dear," Mrs. Bailey suggested after they had moved about half the pile.

"I need a drink. I'll be right back."

Jessa backed down the ladder and headed for the hose. She swallowed the cool, delicious water even though she knew this would mean running all the way to the house to use the toilet. Mrs. Bailey might be right after all. Jessa really hadn't felt totally herself ever since the flu. But that was weeks ago. She couldn't *still* be recovering! All the same, the last time they had moved hay bales, it had been hard work but Jessa certainly hadn't needed a rest halfway through the job.

After one last gulp, Jessa turned off the tap and sprinted up to the house. When she scrambled back up the ladder a few minutes later she felt a bit better. Moving the rest of the hay didn't take long.

"Did you have a good ride today?" Mrs. Bailey was sure trying hard to stay on friendly terms.

Jessa nodded and forced herself to answer. "I took Rebel on a trail ride down past the chicken farm." She didn't add that her plan had been to ride all the way to the sandy beach behind the golf course. Strangely, before she got to Arbutus Road, Jessa had found herself ravenously hungry.

She had finished off the water she carried in her water bottle and headed back to the barn early. The snack of cookies and an apple she wolfed down in the tack room when she'd arrived back at the barn had seemed pitifully small and now, sitting beside Mrs. Bailey in the loft, Jessa was amazed at how hungry she felt again.

"When do you leave for your Rocky Mountain trail ride?"

"I fly out on Sunday afternoon."

"That's the day after tomorrow! You must be excited!"

Jessa nodded and flashed a quick grin at the older woman. It was hard to stay mad at Mrs. Bailey.

"I guess that means you'll be packing on the weekend?"

"I was going to ride on Saturday. . . ."

"But I could call Molly and let her know she can have a lesson on Sunday?"

Jessa sighed and stared at the toe of her gumboot, her fleeting feeling of goodwill dissipating rapidly. *What could she say?* In all likelihood she would still be doing her last-minute packing on Sunday morning. Then she was going to travel to Vancouver on the ferry, and Granny Richardson would pick her up and drop her off at the airport. Mrs. Bailey was right. She wouldn't be able to ride on Sunday.

"I guess so. She won't be jumping, will she?" Perhaps as a result of Jessa's protests, Molly had been staying out of the way on Jessa's riding days. Jessa knew the other girl hadn't stopped riding Rebel, but in the hectic rush of the past weeks, they hadn't run into each other much and Jessa had simply ignored the whole Molly problem.

When Jessa came back from the Rockies, though, things would have to change. During her summer vacation Jessa planned to spend every minute possible down at the barn. Molly would just have to understand that two people couldn't possibly ride one pony at the same time.

Mrs. Bailey patted Jessa's knee. "Don't worry, Jessa. Nothing more exciting than ground poles and maybe some little cross-poles. Nothing Rebel couldn't handle in his sleep. And, only under supervision, of course. Molly's quite a good little rider, you know. She has a natural seat . . . very quiet hands . . ."

"I have to ride Western on the trail ride," Jessa blurted out. She knew it was rude to interrupt, but she couldn't stand to hear another word about Molly's wonderful hands.

The skin around Mrs. Bailey's eyes crinkled into a smile. "Would you like to borrow my cowboy hat?"

"No way!" Jessa looked aghast at Mrs. Bailey's dusty old hat. Mock horror at Jessa's unintended insult froze Mrs. Bailey's face. "I mean, no, thank you."

Mrs. Bailey winked and ran her thumb along the hat brim. "Good. I couldn't do without it. You'll have a wonderful time, I'm sure."

Outside, Jessa's mother's car crunched in the gravel. "I've got to go," she said, jumping up. Without warning, her body sagged and swayed, and she grabbed for a roof strut to keep her balance.

"Hey, are you all right?"

Mrs. Bailey reached out a hand to steady Jessa.

"I'm fine. I just . . . I just stood up too fast, that's all."

As Jessa slowly climbed down the ladder, she couldn't have felt any less fine. Her legs quivered like she'd run three miles at top speed and when she sank into the front seat of the car she was overwhelmed with a desire to sleep. She leaned her head back against the headrest and closed her eyes.

"Are you okay, Jessa?"

"I'm fine. We just moved a bunch of hay. And it's been a busy week."

Jessa's mother smiled. "You can say that again! The last few days of school are always a killer. All that fun is exhausting—sports day, pet day, the awards ceremony . . . well, you can go to bed early tonight and then worry about packing tomorrow. I did two loads of laundry this afternoon, so you have lots of clean T-shirts and socks. . . ."

Her mother's voice took on a strange, distant quality, almost like Jessa was hearing it in a dream. Even though the drive home took less than ten minutes, between the drone of the engine, the warm summer breeze through the open window, and her mother's chatting about final plans and preparations for the trip, she was nearly asleep when they pulled up in front of their little house on Desdemona Street.

Chapter Four

"Jessa!" Granny Richardson clutched Jessa to her ample chest. "My heavens! You've stretched! And skinny as a beanpole! Your mother said she thought you'd lost weight, but my goodness!"

Jessa blushed. Her grandmother was making such a fuss over her, the whole ferry terminal was staring.

"Shall we have some lunch, darling?"

"I'm starving!"

"You're a growing girl, that's why! I certainly hope those cowboys know how to feed you or you'll waste away to nothing! We'll go to Angelino's by the Sea. How does that sound?"

Jessa nodded. She didn't care where they went—she was ravenous.

Waiting for the waitress to take their order at the little restaurant on the waterfront, Jessa gulped down two tall glasses of water.

"They say you should drink eight glasses of water a day, dear. Did you know that?"

Jessa nodded when the waitress offered to fill her glass again. These days, she was drinking three times that much. She figured that must mean she was three times as healthy as anybody else.

The waitress barely had a chance to set Jessa's plate on the table when Jessa plunged her fork into her French fries.

"Didn't you eat breakfast, dear?"

Jessa waited until she had finished her mouthful of fries. "Mom took me out for pancakes and sausages. But that was hours ago."

Granny Richardson smiled and nodded. "Well, you'll put some meat on your bones before long with a healthy appetite like that."

Jessa drained another glass of water and eyed the leftover fries on her grandmother's plate. "Help yourself, dear. I can't possibly eat it all. You may as well fill up now. Who knows when you'll get your next decent meal?"

"Dessert, ladies?"

"Not for me, thank you. Jessa, would you like some ice cream?"

"Yes, please. And another glass of water."

The waitress was back in a few minutes with a big dish of vanilla ice cream.

"We don't have a lot of time to sit and chat—your plane leaves at two o'clock. It would be lovely if you could spend a couple of days with me when you get back."

"Sure," Jessa agreed, scraping the last drop of melted ice cream from the bottom of the glass dish. She considered picking up the bowl and licking the inside clean but thought better of it. Her grandmother wouldn't appreciate such a show of bad manners.

"Well, I suppose we'd better get to the airport. You must be so excited."

Jessa nodded. She knew she should feel excited, but in fact, she felt a bit queasy. Jessa pushed the thought aside. *There was no way she could have the flu again. It wasn't possible.*

"I can't wait," she said, trying to sound enthusiastic. "I'd better stop in the restroom before we leave," she added.

Jessa retreated to the bathroom and leaned against the counter. In the mirror, her cheeks looked flushed and her lips were dry and chapped. She dug in the outside pocket of her shoulder bag and found some lip balm. Her mother was a great packer. She made comprehensive lists and checked everything twice.

Jessa splashed some cool water on her face. Before she straightened up, she cupped her hand under the stream of running water and drank deeply. The flight to Calgary was only an hour and twenty minutes long. She wondered if she could last without having to use the tiny airplane bathroom en route. Not wanting to leave Granny waiting any longer, Jessa sighed, straightened her back, and pushed through the heavy door into the restaurant lobby.

At the airport, Jessa counted and re-counted her bags to make sure she hadn't forgotten anything. She was worn out and she hadn't even left British Columbia!

"You look tired, dear," her grandmother said, straightening one of Jessa's hair clips.

"I was too excited to sleep last night."

"Oh, I know how that is. I'm always afraid I'll sleep through the alarm when I have to travel early in the morning. Maybe you can nap on the plane." Granny Richardson shuddered. "I know it's silly, but I am so scared of flying that I don't dare close my eyes on a plane, even for a moment!"

Jessa smiled. It was odd to think she was braver than her grandmother. Sure, she was a little nervous about her trip, but even the thought of flying terrified her grandmother.

"At the very least, try to get a good night's sleep tonight at the lodge. That way you'll be nice and fresh when you hit the trail in the morning."

Jessa nodded. Her whole body ached and she longed to find a quiet place to stretch out and lie down for a nap. "See you when I get back," she said when Granny Richardson wrapped her in another warm hug.

"Have a wonderful time, dear. I can't wait to hear all about it. Don't forget to take lots and lots of pictures!"

The woman at the airline counter gave Jessa her boarding pass and checked her heavy backpack. Jessa watched her baggage travel along a rumbling black conveyor belt before it disappeared through a suitcase-sized door.

"Through this way, miss," a young man directed, looking at Jessa's ticket.

From the other side of a rope barricade, Granny Richardson waved, kissed the tips of her fingers, and held her hand out towards Jessa. A little embarrassed and with her hands full with her carry-on bags, Jessa could only nod in reply before she disappeared through the doors for passengers.

"Hello. You must be Jessa. My name is Barry."

Jessa bobbed her head at a slim young man wearing the blue uniform of the airline. His long, thin face and sharp nose reminded her of a mouse, though his deep voice seemed to belong to a much larger body.

"Have you ever flown alone before?"

"No. The only time I've ever been on a plane was when I was a baby and my mom took me to Germany, but I don't even remember that." She stopped suddenly, feeling like she had blurted out too much. "No," she repeated. "I've never flown alone."

"Not to worry—it's easy as pie." Jessa followed the back of his blue jacket down the long, sloping ramp that led to the plane.

"Here we are. Welcome aboard! Ellen—this is Jessa."

Jessa smiled at the woman who checked her boarding pass just inside the door of the plane.

"Seat 14-A is a window seat. Welcome aboard."

Everyone was so friendly, Jessa's nervousness about getting lost or boarding the wrong plane quickly dissipated. With so many people watching out for her, it would be difficult to get into any serious trouble. She followed Ellen down the narrow aisle to her seat.

"Let me put your carry-on bag and jacket up here," Ellen said, stowing Jessa's things in the compartment above the seats. "In you get."

Jessa squeezed past a bald man in a dark suit sitting in the seat next to hers. He didn't greet her but rustled his newspaper, Jessa thought a bit impatiently, and disappeared into the news. Once she had settled in her seat and clicked on her seatbelt, a tall, dark-skinned woman with hair swept up into an elegant bun took the aisle seat. The woman's wispy ringlets of hair brushed her cheeks and seemed to be perfectly symmetrical, as if she had carefully measured the size of each coil.

All around Jessa, passengers stuffed coats, bags, and parcels into the overhead bins before finding their seats. A whirr of excitement stirred in her chest and Jessa pressed her nose to the small window beside her. Outside, a baggage car pulling three trailers laden with suitcases and packages zipped past, heading for another plane close by.

Jessa strained to see whether her own bags were being loaded onto her plane, but she couldn't quite see past the wing and engine.

A chime a bit like a doorbell sounded and in the aisle, several flight attendants began a demonstration of how to do up the seatbelt buckles and how oxygen masks would appear if the cabin pressure dropped during the flight. Ellen winked at Jessa when she pulled the sample oxygen mask over her face.

The plane was already taxiing down the runway when the attendants finished pointing out the locations of the emergency exits and toilets, and instructed everyone on board to have a look at the folding safety instruction cards at each seat.

A few minutes later, the plane zoomed down the runway, gathering speed so fast that Jessa was pushed back into her seat. Outside, the grass blurred and then, without warning and when Jessa was beginning to worry that surely they had reached the end of the runway, the nose of the plane tipped up, the wheels left the ground, and the airport fell away beneath them.

With a start, Jessa pulled her head back from the window when the plane was engulfed in a thick, grey cloud and the view completely disappeared.

"Typical," grunted the newspaper man. "You never get to see much flying out of Vancouver."

Jessa leaned back in her seat, fully intending to dig out the Flannigan's brochure to read on the flight, but the drone of the plane numbed her and the next thing she knew, Ellen's hand was on her shoulder, gently waking her up and letting her know they had arrived safely in Calgary.

Chapter Five

The guide from Flannigan's Trail Outfitters was impossible to miss. He was waiting just outside the arrival gate at the Calgary airport and even without the huge Flannigan's sign he was holding, he stuck out of the crowd like a sore thumb. The tall, gangly cowboy looked like he had been peeled right out of a movie scene. His huge ten-gallon hat topped a face weathered and wrinkled from years spent squinting into the sun. Dusty cowboy boots, faded jeans, and a red checked shirt finished off the picture.

"Jessa Richardson?"

Jessa nodded and grinned. Arriving at a strange airport, she had the sudden feeling that she had really gone somewhere, that her adventure had really started. A surge of pure happiness broadened her already wide smile. After her unexpected snooze on the plane, she felt a whole lot better than earlier—well enough to go riding!

"Here, let me help you with your bags. The name's Bill." He tipped his hat and stooped to pluck her bags from the baggage carousel.

"Thank you." Jessa tilted her head back and looked up at him. Bill was tall and lean, but he looked wiry and tough. Three deep furrows splayed out from the corner of each eye. *Laugh lines*, Jessa thought. That's what Granny Richardson called them.

"I hope you don't mind love birds," Bill said, piling her bags onto a luggage cart. Jessa had no idea what he meant.

"Love birds?"

"Better known as Tara and Rick Peterson from Toronto."

"Love birds?" Jessa asked again.

Bill slapped his big hand over his heart. "They're here on their honeymoon. They arrived about an hour ago. I left them in the cafeteria to wait while I came to find you. I'm sure glad you left your husband at home!" He laughed at his own joke with a single, loud "Hah!" and then nudged Jessa. "There they are."

The Petersons weren't hard to pick out. They had snuggled their chairs close together and leaned forward over a map on the table, side by side, their shoulders touching.

Bill cleared his throat and Jessa stifled a giggle.

The Petersons sat up but their hands remained tightly clasped on the table. The young woman spoke first.

"You must be Jessa. Pleased to meet you."

Tara Peterson looked like the least likely person Jessa could imagine going on a riding trip. Her shiny black hair was pulled back neatly into a complicated twist held in place by a sculpted gold clasp. The deep blue-black of her blouse reflected in the deep blue pools of her eyes. Her makeup was perfect, just like the women on the front covers of fashion magazines.

Rick, her husband, looked positively disheveled by comparison. Tara patted at his tousled brown hair as if trying to tame it into shape and absently, smoothed at the front of his rumpled green polo shirt. Though he didn't look like the male equivalent of his model wife, Rick didn't look much like a cowboy, either.

"Time to go, folks," Bill said, nodding at their over-loaded luggage cart. Rick folded away the map and the couple stood up, holding hands. It really did seem like they were glued together and couldn't move independently. It took a bit of organizing for them to be able to manage their baggage cart and hand luggage and still keep their fingers intertwined. Jessa was so distracted with their antics and Bill's goofy faces, she nearly forgot to make a pit stop.

"Excuse me, I'd better go to the bathroom before we go," Jessa said. She was getting accustomed to planning to use facilities whenever they were available.

Bill shepherded his passengers into a minivan emblazoned with a colourful painting of horses winding along a high mountain trail.

"May I be so bold as to ask what this is?" he asked, manipulating a long package into the back of the van.

"My easel," Tara said.

"My wife's an artist," Rick added proudly.

Bill didn't comment, but Jessa thought she caught a bemused look pass over his leathery face.

Soon after they pulled away from the airport, the flat, sprawling fields of the prairies began to roll over gently undulating hills. The farms here were quite different from those Jessa was used to at home.

"Is that all wheat?" Tara asked.

Bill grunted. "Mostly. Lots of grazing land, too. Cattle and ostrich."

"Ostrich?" Rick squawked.

"Mostly cattle. Some ranchers are experimenting with other livestock—ostrich, emu, llamas."

The three passengers peered eagerly out the windows, hoping to catch a glimpse of something exotic, but Alberta had hardly become a wildlife game park for foreign animals. The only living creatures Jessa spotted were stocky brown and white beef cattle and the occasional small herd of horses, heads down, grazing on the early summer growth of rich grass.

"Too bad we won't have ostrich steaks at the barbecue tonight. Ostrich meat is very tasty! You'll just have to make do with juicy Alberta beef steaks and roasted corn on the cob."

Then, it seemed the foothills were no longer hills but, without warning, muscled up into mountains.

Tara and Rick sighed appreciatively at the changing landscape.

"Is that snow up there?" Tara asked.

"At the top of the mountains or in shade pockets, there's snow all year round," Bill explained.

Despite the craggy peaks that grew more impressive with each turn of the road, the hum of the engine had a hypnotic effect on Jessa. Bill's voice describing the others who would be going on the trail ride ("Adam and Dianne—they're from Florida . . . drove all the way to the lodge . . . quite a trip . . .") lulled her to sleep and she didn't stir again until the front doors of the van slammed and the others scrambled out in the gravel parking lot in front of Flannigan's Lodge.

"Have a good sleep?" Bill asked.

Jessa nodded, though her head felt thick and heavy. Two naps in one day? Travel was more tiring than she had anticipated.

She climbed out after the others and stretched in the afternoon sunshine. The lodge was a large, impressive log building with huge windows reaching two stories high. The wall of windows faced a spectacular view of the Rocky Mountains.

Jessa turned in a slow circle, gawking at the snow-tipped peaks towering around them. It was hard to imagine where, exactly, they would be riding since the mountains seemed covered with impenetrable woods on their lower slopes, and impassable cliffs higher up.

Bill's quick descriptions of where they should take their bags ("in through the lobby and up the stairs . . . your names are on the guest-room doors"), where to meet for dinner, and where to find the bathrooms reminded Jessa how badly she had to go—again! By the time she had staggered up the stairs, heaved her bags onto her bed, and found the bathroom down the hall, tears of desperation stung in her eyes.

What was going on? She wondered if maybe she had a bladder infection or if her kidneys weren't working properly, but pushed the thought away. *People didn't die from bladder infections. She was in Alberta now and couldn't do anything about it anyway. Maybe whatever the problem was would just clear up by itself.*

As she washed her hands and then took a long drink from the faucet, she promised herself that when she got back to Kenwood, she would go to the doctor just in case something was wrong. Until then, she was going to have a great time, starting with dinner.

On the drive through the mountains, Bill had promised, "The mountain air will make you hungry like you've never been before." Bill was right. From somewhere in the building, delicious smells wafted through the air, making Jessa's mouth water. She followed the aromas downstairs.

Bill's easy banter never stopped as all the guests gathered around a large, outdoor fire pit to eat. Introductions were made quickly. "Adam and Dianne are here from Fort Lauderdale in Florida; Melanie is from California; Jessa from British Columbia; and Tara and Rick from the big T-O." Each guest nodded politely in turn.

"There are only six of you on this ride—usually we take eight to ten up at a time, but this early in the year only the toughest make the trip."

Tara's blue eyes widened.

"Russell, here," all the guests turned to look at a skinny young man wearing chaps, cowboy boots, and a hat so big it seemed to swallow his whole head, "Russ doesn't like guiding the first trip of the year. It's hard to get the campers out of their tents on snowy mornings."

"Snow?" Tara squeezed Rick's hand, and her eyes grew even bigger.

"I don't mind the snow—we don't generally get much this time of year," the younger cowboy said. "It's the bears that make me nervous."

Jessa exchanged a worried look with Melanie, the middle-aged woman from California. Melanie's lips mouthed a horrified *Bears?*

"Now, Russell, it's not polite to scare the guests."

Though Bill winked broadly and then licked his fingers as if he hadn't a care in the world beyond finishing his dinner, he didn't deny that snow and bears were possible hazards.

"Can we meet our horses after dinner?" Jessa asked, surprising herself with her bravery but anxious to change the subject. She wasn't used to being alone with a group of grown-ups she didn't know.

"You've been reading the schedule!" Bill said, grinning. "Take your plates to the kitchen—that door beyond the hot tub. The woman with the short, black hair and the tattoo is Bing. She's our cook here at the lodge. Be nice to her or she'll poison you." Bill slapped Russ on the back and the two jovial cowboys stood, indicating the meal had come to an end.

Jessa saw Bing's tattoo when she handed the cook her empty plate. A grinning snake wrapped down her forearm and around her wrist. The snake's wide mouth chomped down on its own tail, making a slightly scary bracelet. When Jessa looked into the woman's round face, she was relieved to see a pair of sparkling grey-green eyes and a big smile.

"Carrot?"

At first, Jessa thought the cook was offering her more to eat. She was about to refuse when Bing added, "For your horse! Never hurts to bribe them a little."

Bing laughed and her ample bosom shook. She wiped her hands on her apron and handed each guest a carrot. The snake's eyes seemed to turn with the movements of her wrist as she passed out the treats.

"Have fun!" she called out as the group retreated down the hill leading to the horse corrals. Bing looked tough with her three glittering earrings in each ear and pierced nose to boot, but Jessa decided she liked the friendly, tattooed cook.

Chapter Six

"This is Spirit. Your partner for the week."

The Appaloosa gelding pushed his nose through the rails of the corral. Jessa offered him the carrot, glad to have come bearing a treat.

Bill watched Spirit munching on the carrot. "If you're nice to Bing, she always has special treats for you and your horse."

Jessa wasn't sure she wanted to know what Bing might do if someone wasn't nice to her. She reached over the fence and scratched her new friend under his long, tangled mane. "Can I brush him?" she asked.

"Sure. He'd like that." Bill showed her which of several halters belonged to Spirit. "You can tie him up over here at the hitching rail. You know how to tie a safety knot?"

Jessa nodded. She let herself into the corral where Spirit and several other horses dozed. Her gelding was quiet and she led him easily to the nearby rail and tied him up.

With horse brushes in her hands, Jessa felt better than she had so far during her trip. Whisking the stiff bristles over his spotted coat, she relaxed as she flicked at the swirls of dried mud on his back.

"You had a good roll, didn't you?" she said softly.

Spirit shifted his weight and one of his hind feet tilted forward until only the tip of the toe was resting on the ground. The dainty position always reminded her of ballet dancers.

Jessa dug in her pocket for the sugar cubes she had sneaked into her pocket at dinner.

"You're probably not allowed to have these," she said, looking around to make sure she was alone before offering the treat to her horse. He lipped the white cubes from her open palm and crunched the illegal treats happily. "Next time, I'll ask for more carrots," she promised.

Jessa picked up the brushes and resumed the rhythmic brush strokes.

"Spirit's never looked so good," Bill crooned when he came to check on Jessa a short time later. "Here come the Petersons now. Looks like Mrs. P. had to get changed! Jessa, can you do me a favour and help me show them how to handle a horse on the ground? Between you and me, those two are real greenhorns."

The cowboy winked at Jessa and ran his big hand over Spirit's rump. "Spirit's a good boy. I think you two will get along just fine. He'll appreciate someone with a little horse sense."

Jessa grinned and then nodded towards the newlyweds, who were picking their way, hand in hand, down the path to the corrals. Tara may have changed clothes, but she hardly looked better prepared to get close to a dusty horse. Her pale blue jeans hugged her hips. A white blouse, vaguely reminiscent of Western style but considerably cleaner, was topped off with a bright red kerchief tied neatly around the woman's neck. It was all Jessa could do not to laugh, especially when she saw Bill bite his lower lip and stare hard at the ground until he had regained his composure.

"Tara! Rick! I was just chatting with Jessa here about the finer points of horse handling. You ready to meet your ponies?" It seemed the cowboys referred to their mounts as ponies regardless of the horses' size. At the other end of the corrals, Russ was helping Melanie and the two guests from Florida brush their horses.

Tara nodded. "Honey, look at that pretty spotted one." She pointed at Spirit, but Jessa noticed that her other hand still clung to Rick's.

"That's Spirit, Jessa's horse. The one over there with the red halter is yours, ma'am." Bill gestured towards a large palomino.

"And the dun is yours, Rick."

"Dun?"

"The brownish one. Her name is Dusty."

"What's mine called?" Tara asked.

"Tony Maloney."

Bill caught the two horses and led them over to the hitching rail where he tied them up, one on either side of Spirit.

"Jessa here will show you how to brush them. She's a regular expert."

Jessa smiled awkwardly. She noticed the way Bill had separated the horses. Now the two lovebirds would have to let go of each other!

"How many horses will be going tomorrow?" Rick asked.

"Twelve altogether. Six guests and two guides."

"And twelve horses?" Tara asked. For a minute, Jessa couldn't see how the numbers added up either.

"Four pack horses."

"Oh, of course." Tara smiled uneasily and Jessa got the distinct impression the elegant young woman from Toronto was not entirely comfortable with the whole idea of heading out into the wilderness on horseback. She wondered why on earth the pair had chosen a wilderness trail ride as their honeymoon destination rather than a luxurious resort in Hawaii or the south of France. Rick picked up a soft brush and swiped awkwardly at Dusty's scraggly mane. Tara hung back, staring at the brushes in her hands.

"Here, start over on this side," Jessa said, moving to Tony Maloney's left side. "Start with this stiffer brush and follow the direction of the hair. That's pretty good. You can brush harder. Sort of flick the brush a bit to get the dust out of his coat."

Bill hadn't gone far. He leaned casually against the split rail fence, one boot resting on the bottom rail. He winked encouragingly at Jessa.

At first, Jessa thought Tara was going to balk at brushing her dusty horse. But after a few minutes, the city slicker was brushing away like an expert, though she did try to stand as far away as possible to avoid dirtying her white shirt. Jessa noticed that Rick had switched to his stiff brush and was also vigorously grooming Dusty.

Jessa heard oohs and aahs and laughter from the other group as they admired each other's horses and their fine grooming jobs. She showed the couple from Toronto how to hold their hoofpicks. Grooming the three horses took ten times longer than normal but when they finally finished, the horses looked gorgeous and the newlyweds looked exceedingly pleased with themselves. Jessa stifled a feeling of smug satisfaction when she noticed a long smudge of dirt reaching from Tara's shoulder right down the front of her blouse and ending with a broad smear on the woman's brand new jeans.

"Thanks for all your help, Jessa," Tara smiled as they led their horses back to the corral.

Jessa grinned back but suddenly felt very tired. The smile faded from her lips and she could hardly walk up the short hill to the lodge for hot chocolate and oatmeal cookies.

Though she longed to slip away to bed after she had

wolfed down four cookies, a mug of hot chocolate, and two large glasses of water, the evening's activities were not yet finished.

The six guests sank comfortably into large couches and armchairs arranged in front of the massive granite fireplace in a grand, oversized "living room." Though a fire crackled merrily in the grate, everyone's attention was fixed on a most peculiar contraption. Suspended from the heavy, open beams above them was a round oil drum. The fat barrel hung from two stout ropes, one fastened to either end. Strapped onto the barrel was a Western saddle.

"What do you suppose that's for?" Dianne asked nobody in particular. Bill heard her question as he entered the big room and answered with another of his short, barking laughs.

"Can't have riding lessons out there in the dark now, can we?" he said. "That's why we have old Barney here."

The whites of Adam's eyes flashed against his deep Floridian tan. "You've got to be joking!"

"Joking? Me? Pull your leg?"

Nobody dared answer.

"Okay—more properly I guess this should be called a 'mounting up and basics of steering lesson.' Who wants to go first? Come on—don't be shy! It's not like this old guy is going to take off on you." The barrel clanked as the old cowboy swatted the pretend horse on the flank. The whole contraption swayed slightly from side to side.

Rick tugged Tara's arm into the air to volunteer her, but she glared at him and pulled her arm away.

Dianne stood up slowly. "I guess I'll go and get it over with."

Bill beamed and whacked her on the back. "Atta girl!"

Dianne looked very small beside the swinging barrel,

which was raised to about the same height as a sixteen-hand horse.

"Other side," Bill instructed, suddenly all business. "Always mount up from the near side—that's the horse's left."

The woman eyed the barrel warily. "Now what?"

A piercing whistle was the answer. Bill took his fingers from his mouth and waved Russell into the room. The younger cowboy had a Western headstall draped over his neck and held a bit in his hands.

"Get over here, Russy. Good boy!"

Russell, dutifully trying to look horse-like, took his place in front of the barrel. He looked more than a little foolish. The guests' efforts to be polite were failing miserably. Soon everyone was laughing at poor Dianne's efforts to hold Russy's reins and reach up for the saddle horn, all the while keeping her left foot in the near-side stirrup.

"It's moving!" Dianne protested weakly through her worsening giggles. She hopped about on her right foot as the barrel swung more and more vigorously from side to side. When her "horse" tossed his head and pulled the reins from her hand, she gave up and stepped back, still laughing.

"Do you think horses are always going to stand still for you?" Even though Bill's words were stern, when Bing came into the room from the kitchen to investigate all the hoots and howls of laughter, he didn't stop her from holding the barrel still for Dianne.

One by one, each would-be cowboy took a turn mounting the ornery barrel. And, as each climbed aboard (some more gracefully than others), Bill gave them a quick rundown on Western riding.

"Left hand only on the reins, Jessa. You English riders are all the same. You have to neck rein—like this." He showed her how to move her hand from side to side and lay the reins across the horse's neck to indicate the turn direction. Russell obediently moved in the right direction when Jessa gave the aids correctly.

"What if the horse runs away?" Tara asked on her turn.

Bill wiggled the barrel back and forth quite wildly and Tara instinctively grabbed for the saddle horn with both hands. Her shrill shriek made everyone jump. Bill slowed the "runaway" and put his big hand over Tara's on the horn.

"Grabbing hold is a good thing—but don't drop your reins. Your horse isn't likely to run off. We've matched you with a very quiet horse who will just follow along. But if old Tony Maloney gets going faster than a plod, pull back on the reins like this and with your other hand hang onto the saddle horn real tight."

Tara didn't look at all relieved after hearing his instructions but shook her head anyway when Bill asked if she had any more questions.

Once everyone had had a go and was settled back into the couches, the laughter quieted down and Bill unfastened the throat latch where it had been fastened under Russell's armpits.

"Any more questions? No? Good. Tomorrow after breakfast we'll help you get mounted on your real, live horses and then you can all have a little riding practice in the big corral before we set off. You'll be fine, Tara. Guaranteed."

Russell cleared his throat.

"Can we hoist up old Barney?"

Bill nodded and he and Russell pulled on ropes looped through pulleys fastened to the beams above and hauled the barrel way up into the rafters. At last, it was time for bed.

On her way to her room Jessa carefully double-checked the exact route she would have to take to get to the bathroom during the night. And then, with hardly a chance to think about the fact she was hundreds of miles from home and lying in a strange bed about to embark on a great adventure, she sank into a deep sleep.

Jessa struggled to hang onto the dream images dissipating rapidly into the darkness. In the dream she had felt warm and happy as she rode Spirit along Desdemona Street back in Kenwood. Her hands were filled with rosy apples and every few steps she leaned forward and fed one to her horse. She could have stayed in that dream forever. Instead, she was overwhelmed with a need to tiptoe down the hallway to use the facilities. She sighed and sat up slowly to get her bearings. *Out the door and to the left . . .*

She crept out of bed, surprised to find her legs shaky and weak, and made her way out into the hallway. She checked the sign on the bathroom door to make sure she was going into the right room. It would have been very embarrassing to have walked in on a sleeping guest by mistake.

On her way out of the bathroom, she hesitated in front of the sink and then glanced at her watch. *Three-thirty!* The wake-up call was supposed to be at seven. *Surely she could last three and a half hours!* With a sigh, she turned on the tap and leaned over the sink to drink.

Chapter Seven

"How far will we ride today?" The new Mrs. Peterson poured her husband another cup of coffee. "Will we make it to Skoki Lake today?"

"Not too far. About fifteen miles." Bill winked at Jessa and handed her the platter of pancakes. "We won't get to Skoki Lake until tomorrow. We make camp partway there tonight."

"So, Bill, do you think we can manage Tara's easel?" Rick chose a fluffy pancake and put it on Tara's plate with a smile.

"I'm sure we can. Remember the time that astronomer brought his telescope?"

Russ joined the group for breakfast. He snorted as he recalled a trip he had led a few years earlier. Jessa thought he sounded a bit like a horse when he laughed. She wondered if that was why he was the one who had to pretend to be a horse during the riding lessons.

"I remember, all right. What with the tripod and the spare lenses and all those reference books—I thought we'd have to bring along another horse just to manage."

"Or a camel," Bill chuckled. "He sure had a lot of equipment."

"And he insisted every single piece was critical."

"Funniest thing was, he was having such a good time singing songs at the campfire and chugging back hot chocolate I don't think he looked at the stars once!"

Russ slapped his thigh. "That's right! Until the last night, remember? Then he unpacked all that gear and got himself all set up and then it clouded right over!"

Bill whooped. "I thought the poor professor was going to start crying!"

"Well, I intend to paint every day," Tara declared, sounding a little put out by the joking cowboys.

"Oh, I'm sure you will, ma'am. No disrespect intended." Bill winked at Russ who quickly jumped in and agreed.

"Inspiration is easy to find up here in the mountains," he grinned.

"That's why we're here," Rick added, squeezing his hand over the top of his wife's. Tara smiled at him and leaned over to give him a quick kiss on the cheek. "Tara has always wanted to do a series of mountain paintings. This trip seemed like a golden opportunity."

So, that was why they had chosen such an unlikely honeymoon. Jessa groaned inwardly as she watched the swooning couple. She promised herself that no matter what, she would never behave like such a mush-monster in public!

"Couldn't ask for much better weather for setting out, eh, Russ?"

"Helluva lot better than the year it snowed—remember that? First weekend in July and it looked like a Christmas card!"

The Petersons looked outside, as if to make sure the weather hadn't suddenly changed, and sighed appreciatively. The big windows of the lodge dining room tried to frame an unframable view. The mountains outside could not be contained, but speared up into the sky, filling the room with their presence. Jessa wondered how anyone could possibly paint such overwhelming magnificence.

"Do you ever get tired of that view?" Dianne asked.

Russ pursed his lips, tipped his chair back onto two legs, and shook his head.

"Probably because it's never the same twice."

Today, the snow still lying high on the mountain peaks looked like white icing, spread smoothly over the towering, granite crags.

"Ever feel claustrophobic?"

"Nope. But sometimes tourists complain that they feel hemmed in. Especially if they're from flat places like Florida."

Dianne blushed and pushed her plate back. "Well, that was a delicious stack of pancakes! Was that real Canadian maple syrup?"

"Absolutely!" grinned Bill. "Nothing but the finest around here. Now, if you'll excuse us, we have lots to do. Russ?"

"I'm ready." Russ shovelled the last bite of pancake into his mouth, guzzled the rest of his coffee, and pushed back his chair.

Bill stopped at the dining room door. "Tara, I noticed you have three duffel bags. You'll need to make a few decisions. One bag is the limit—we want our pack horses to last all summer."

Now it was Tara's turn to blush. "One bag for a whole week?" From the pained look on her face, choosing which outfits would be appropriate would be a difficult chore.

"When everyone is packed, bring your duffel bags down to the corrals. Russ and I are going to get the pack horses ready. As you finish, come on down and join us. You can groom your own horses and then we'll help you saddle up. Then you can ride around a bit in the big corral. Everything clear?"

Heads nodded around the table and then everyone scattered to get ready.

On the stairs leading to the guest rooms, Jessa fell into step with Melanie, the woman from California.

"You're so lucky to live in Canada," Melanie said. "It's so incredibly beautiful here. And clean."

Jessa thought that was a funny thing to say, but she nodded anyway to be polite.

"Are there mountains where you live in British Columbia?" Melanie asked.

"Not like this. Mostly it's very green with lots of trees where I come from—I live on the southern part of Vancouver Island. I can see the ocean from near where I live—I ride my horse to the beach sometimes."

Melanie sighed like someone in a movie who has fallen in love.

Her sigh was contagious and Jessa was surprised a little by the longing she heard in her own voice. "I wish I could go to California one day. You have real sand beaches there, and warm water, and Disneyland."

"Aren't we silly?" Melanie laughed. "We always seem to want something other than what we have. Lots of Canadians visit California and look where I am for my vacation! To me, California is just boring old home! See you in a bit," she added, and they disappeared into their rooms.

Sounds of shuffling, sorting, and zipping could soon be heard in the various guest rooms.

"What do you think—the blue shirt or the white one?" Jessa heard Tara ask.

"Blue's more practical," Rick suggested.

"What about my paints? Will they have room for my paints?"

Jessa stuffed her towel into her duffel bag and zipped the bag closed. Her mother had stuck closely to the suggested packing list. For once Jessa was glad her mother was so particular—Jessa had no tough decisions to make.

She heaved her own bag down to the corral and then went back to the lodge for her day pack. By then, Rick was struggling down the stairs with two very large bags.

"Those are the biggest duffel bags I've ever seen!" Bill declared when they arrived at the designated mustering area.

"I left two bags in our room!" Tara said. "Will our stuff be safe here while we're gone?"

"Not to worry—nobody else will be using the lodge while we're away."

"Do we need to try to leave something else behind?" Rick offered, ignoring Tara's alarmed look.

Bill held up his hand. "We'll manage. We'll use Hercules."

Hercules was appropriately named. The gelding was massive, more like a small draft horse than anything someone might ride.

"And my easel?"

"Yes, ma'am. We'll find a way to take the easel."

Jessa wondered if she was imagining a gruff edge creeping into Bill's usually cheerful voice.

The cowboy turned back to loading the pack horses. As the duffel bags arrived, Bill and Russ piled the gear in neat heaps balanced on top of large, outspread tarps. When the piles all looked about the right size, they fastened ropes around each bundle then lifted the tarp corners and folded them over as if they were wrapping gigantic Christmas presents.

Each pack horse wore a strange wooden saddle that looked a bit like a mini-sawhorse. It quickly became obvious that the tarp parcels were tied onto the pack saddles. The cowboys lashed one bundle on each side of a pack horse, making sure the loads were equally heavy on both sides. A long rope looped over and around the bundles. Russ tied off the end securely and gave the horse a firm pat on the neck.

Bing, the cook, was busy loading tins and small sacks

into two large, wooden boxes.

"Are you coming with us?" Jessa asked.

"Nope," Bing said, tucking a plastic container of peanut butter into one of the boxes. "On the fourth day I'll ride up with some fresh supplies. The boys will be doing all the cooking until then."

Bill caught Jessa curiously eyeing the equipment.

"This is Bella," he said, gesturing to a black mare tied beside the boxes. She's the quietest, most sure-footed horse we've got. That's why she has the special honour of being the kitchen horse. We can make do without just about anything else, but we won't get far without grub. Right, Jessa?"

Jessa grinned. She knew the old cowboy was teasing her about her healthy appetite. The weight of her day pack was suddenly heavy on her back. Though she knew Bill had given her his personal assurance that there would be lots of food, she had packed extra cookies, crackers, a bag of raisins, and a water bottle in her day pack, just in case she couldn't wait for the rest breaks. Bill had helped her sweet-talk Bing into parting with the bag of raisins and the cookies.

While Russ and Bill worked with the horses, Bing finished packing the food. When she was done, she directed traffic as the greenhorns caught their horses. Jessa was by far the most knowledgeable of the group and was recruited to help the others with grooming. She smiled when she heard Rick telling Dianne and Adam that they should start with a stiff brush and work first on the horse's left side.

Spirit was filthy again, despite Jessa's efforts from the night before. Obviously, he was a horse who liked to roll, apparently in the muddiest corner of the corral. Jessa worked fast, eager to be in the saddle.

"Can I help you with Betty Bay?" she asked Dianne, who was struggling to pry a small rock free from her horse's hoof.

"It's jammed right in the corner here. I don't want to jab her foot."

"Here, let me try." Jessa set to work, firmly working out the troublesome rock from where it had wedged in towards the back of the bay mare's frog. "There you go!" she said, gently putting down Betty Bay's hoof and giving her a pat on the shoulder.

"Thanks. Do you think she's clean enough?"

Jessa eyed the mare's dusty brown coat. "No offence, but not really. I'll help you."

Jessa set to work, brushing vigorously until clouds of dust hung in the air above the horse.

"I didn't know you could brush so hard . . . I didn't want to hurt her."

Far from looking troubled, Betty Bay seemed to be thoroughly enjoying the good grooming. Her eyes half closed and she leaned into Jessa's confident brush strokes.

"Did you get the easel?" Tara called out.

"Yes'm. You'll have to wait until we're at the Pipestone Creek camp to use it. We've wrapped it in with the sleeping bags."

"That's okay. I have my sketchbook in my day pack. I'll do some sketches at lunchtime."

"This is heavy!" Jessa exclaimed when she reached to grab the big Western saddle from the rail.

"No wimpy little excuses for saddles like you English folks use!" grinned Bing. She helped Jessa settle the saddle onto two thick saddle pads. Jessa reached under Spirit's belly and caught the big ring on the end of the string girth. It didn't look anything like the girth on her saddle at home. There were no buckles, no way to fasten it that Jessa could see.

Now it was her turn to feel like a greenhorn.

"You take the ring of the cinch like this," explained Bing, taking the ring from Jessa. "Then you feed this latigo through here like this—through the top ring of the girth, then you tie it off like this."

"No buckles?"

"No buckles. You probably don't use a breast collar or a breech strap, either."

Jessa watched Bing fasten the extra equipment front and back.

The cook pulled Spirit's tail over the crupper. "This will stop the saddle from sliding forward when you're going down steep hills. And this," she said, tapping the breast collar, "will help stop the saddle from sliding backwards when you're going uphill. Spirit's a good horse, but as you probably noticed, he doesn't have much in the way of withers. That can make it hard to keep everything where it's supposed to be."

The sun was high by the time all the gear had been packed and secured on the horses and all the guests were settled aboard their mounts and ready to go. Judging by the rather hopeless steering Jessa had witnessed in the big corral, it was a relief to find out the horses knew their jobs so well.

"They'll just follow along," Bill reassured Tara. "If you have real trouble, we can always slip a halter on old Tony and lead him. But I'm sure you'll be fine—we've had six-year-olds do this trip."

"Let's go!" Russ called from the front of the line. He led two pack horses behind him. Melanie fell in behind the second pack horse. Her rangy chestnut, Stewart, balked for a minute and only moved on when Bing gave him a slap on the rump. Both Melanie and Stewart looked a little surprised. Rick and Tara were next, followed by Jessa, Adam, and then Dianne on Betty Bay. Bill, on his solid black gelding Blaster, brought up the rear with his string of two pack horses.

"Have a great time!" Bing called with a wave.

A chorus of farewells and goodbyes echoed off the mountain slopes.

"Don't forget to bring chocolate when you come!" Dianne joked.

Spirit moved out willingly but without seeming at all excited. The trail was dry and gravelly where it led away from the corrals and through a path flanked by pine trees. Her horse's steady swaying gait, the crinch and crunch of the horses' hooves against the dry trail, and the warmth of the sun soon lulled Jessa into a state of total relaxation.

If she could spend her whole life, every day, just like this, she would be happy. A flash of black and white darted past her in the trees.

"What was that?" Dianne asked.

"Magpie," Bill answered.

The trail angled down across the face of a fairly steep embankment.

"Lean back! Right back—that's it!" Bill shouted instructions to the green riders from the back of the line.

Russ looked back over his shoulder to see how the others were doing as the horses picked their way down the trail.

"Give them their heads—that's it . . . relax . . . lean back."

Spirit's hind end came under nicely as he began the descent, and Jessa leaned back, freeing his front end to find a safe way down through the loose footing. It was hard to remember to hold her reins in her left hand like the guides, but she forced her right hand to rest loosely on her thigh or on the top of the saddle horn.

In every direction the mountains scraped up against the sky—vaguely menacing, huge and immovable. At the bottom of the embankment, water splashed and danced over boulders and stones. The water level was low enough that the horses made their way along the stream without getting wet.

After about fifteen minutes, Russ stopped and raised his hand.

"We're going to cross here," he said.

"What if they slip?" Tara asked.

"Then you'll get wet!"

Jessa noticed that not everybody laughed at Russ's joke.

"You'll be fine. Tony boy has been through this creek dozens of times. He could do it blindfolded. The water is barely up to their knees. Just give him a little extra rein and let him find his way."

Russ swung around in the saddle. "Let them drink as we go through—they shouldn't be too thirsty yet, but it's fine if they have a little water here."

Darlin' must have heard her rider because just as he spoke, she stretched her neck down and took a long swig. She lifted her head and trickles of water dribbled from her chin. She smacked her lips together and then stepped calmly into the water.

Several of the others also stopped for a drink, but Spirit just moseyed on through the gurgling water, completely oblivious to the splashing droplets flinging up every which way.

Unfortunately, all that running water reminded Jessa just how thirsty she was. Once they had settled back into a steady walk on the other side of the stream, she wriggled her day pack off her shoulder and eased it around into her lap. Spirit paid no attention whatsoever to the rustling noises coming from the person on his back. Jessa fished out her water bottle and squirted the liquid into her mouth.

The horses continued to pick their way along the trail in the high mountain valley. Spring wildflowers dotted the lower slopes of the mountains. Every now and then the guides would stop so the riders could snap photographs of the glorious views.

By noon, just as Jessa was beginning to think she couldn't go another step without eating something, Russ pulled up in a clearing overlooking a river not far below.

The riders dismounted and spread out. Jessa slipped on Spirit's halter and hooked his bridle over her saddle horn as Russ and Bill had instructed. Several of the others needed help with the equipment change. Jessa sat in the grass and kept a firm hold on the end of Spirit's lead shank. Her horse eagerly attacked the grass.

"You're hungry, too, aren't you?" she murmured so only he could hear her.

She grinned appreciatively when Bill brought her a peanut butter and jelly sandwich from one of the wooden boxes on Bella's side. As she munched away happily, she noticed that Tara had left her horse in Rick's care and taken her lunch to the very edge of the clearing. She was sketching the sweep of the valley with one hand and holding a giant oatmeal cookie with the other.

"There's an outhouse just over behind those trees, for anyone who needs it," Bill said cheerily. "We'll be mounting up in ten minutes. We're still a couple of hours away from camp."

Jessa had already located the outhouse, but decided she had better use it again. When she returned, the cowboys had packed away the lunch things. The riders stretched and had a final gaze at the glorious vista before them.

After lunch, everyone seemed quieter. The easy chatter of the morning had stopped and Jessa wondered why. She figured out the silence of the grown-ups when Tara said, "How much farther? My . . . my backside is a little . . ."

"Tender?" Russ asked with a quick wink over his shoulder.

Tara and several of the others nodded. Jessa grinned to herself. So that was the problem—the greenhorns were saddle sore!

Chapter Eight

"There's the camp!"

"Thank goodness!" Dianne remarked, looking down from the ridge where Bill had stopped. Down below, tucked into the inside of a bend in the river, several large tents stood in a circle. Everyone was happy to see their destination!

"How are we going to get over there?" Rick asked as the group began to pick their way down the steep hill towards the valley floor. "Where's the bridge?"

"Bridge?" Russ snorted. "We're going to ford the river."

"What!" Melanie sounded horrified. "We have to swim?"

"No ma'am. The horses are going to wade across. This time of year the water doesn't quite reach their bellies. We'll cross at a low point a little upstream from camp."

"What if Tony Maloney falls over?" Tara sounded more than a little nervous.

"Not to worry—these horses know what they're doing."

Despite Bill's reassuring words, even Jessa found herself eyeing the river nervously. It looked a lot bigger and more dangerous the closer they drew. By the time they were following the trail along the river's edge, it looked more like something to be navigated on a whitewater raft than on horseback. No longer did the river look like a picturesque part of a landscape painting. Now it loomed before them like a dangerous obstacle only fools would tackle on horseback.

"Here's where we'll cross. Let your horses stop for a drink before you start. Keep your eyes ahead or look upstream. Don't look downstream—you might get dizzy and fall off and we don't want to rescue anyone! The water is mighty cold!"

Jessa swallowed nervously. Spirit followed the others and stepped calmly into the swirling water. He stretched down and had a long drink. Jessa felt the current tugging at his legs. She looked down at the water gurgling and pulling beneath them and immediately regretted it.

"Jessa, look upstream!" Bill shouted from behind her. Spirit's knees disappeared into the water and Jessa could feel the increasing effort her horse had to make as he pushed his way into the river.

The water lapped at the underneath of her stirrups. Jessa's heart thudded a mile a minute. What if her horse stumbled? She would pitch head first over his shoulder and be swept away downstream, never to be seen again! Her knuckles turned white on the saddle horn.

"Give him a nudge, there, Jessa! Keep him moving."

Jessa squeezed her legs to Spirit's sides. What if Bill and Russ had miscalculated the depth of the water? Surely any moment the water would be over their heads? What if Spirit fell into an invisible underwater hole?

The far bank didn't seem to be getting any closer. Jessa risked a quick look back over her shoulder. They were right out in the middle of the river now, the water tickling her horse's belly, pouring down around them, threatening to sweep him right off his feet.

Spirit didn't seem at all perturbed. He kept on going, pushing steadily against the water. Gradually, the water level began to go down and he sped up as it became easier to ford the shallows. He bounded the last few steps out of the water and up the bank on the far side.

"Hang on now, Jessa, in case he—"

Bill didn't have a chance to finish his sentence. Spirit shook himself like a dog and tossed his head.

Still clutching the horn, Jessa giggled with relief. They had made it! A moment later all the others scrambled up the riverbank and then the whole group turned and headed down towards camp.

"You'll be in this tent with Melanie."

Bill tossed Jessa's duffel bag onto her canvas camp cot. The tents were large and roomy enough to accommodate two cots and lots of gear. "You can unpack while we whip something up for dinner."

"Oh, my aching backside!" Melanie moaned as she sank onto her cot. "Aren't you stiff?"

Jessa shook her head. "Just hungry."

"Me, too. I wonder what's for dinner?"

The riders didn't have to wait long. Obviously the two cowboys appreciated the way riders worked up an appetite in the great outdoors. It didn't take long for Melanie and Jessa to arrange their sleeping bags, pull out sweaters, and join the others around the fire pit. Already a fire was crackling away and Bill was organizing the camp kitchen.

While Bill cooked, Russ tended to the horses. He made sure everyone had fresh hay, grain, and water in the makeshift rope corrals close by.

Before long, sausages sizzled on the grill, and puffy biscuits heated in a heavy cast-iron pan. Slathered with gravy and sitting on top of steaming baked beans, the biscuits tasted scrumptious. Fresh fruit, giant cookies, hot chocolate, and marshmallows finished off the tasty mountain meal.

"Excellent," sighed Rick, leaning back against a big rock conveniently positioned near the fire.

"Anyone for chocolate cake?"

Several riders groaned and patted their stomachs, but everyone accepted a piece of the chocolate layer cake Bill produced from one of the kitchen boxes.

"I'm so full I can hardly move," Dianne sighed. "I'm going for a little walk along the river—anyone want to come?"

"Watch out for grizzlies," Russ remarked.

"Really?"

"Make lots of noise and stay out of their way. You'll be fine."

Heads swivelled as everyone tried to spot bears heading for the campsite. Bill chuckled. "Don't worry," he said. "They don't usually come right into camp. We bury garbage we can't burn in a couple of metal boxes up over the ridge, and then we pack it out again at the end of the trip. Don't keep any food in your tents, though. And, if any of your bags had food in it, give it to us and we'll hang it for you. Even if you take the food out, the scent lingers. We have a bear-safe cache set up for stuff we don't want eaten before we have a chance to get to it ourselves."

Bill looked right at Jessa when he mentioned the food-filled bags. She made a mental note to bring him her day pack right away so no food smells lingered in her tent. That's all she needed—a midnight visit from a hungry grizzly bear!

Later that evening, when the campers were recovering around the campfire from their day's ride, Bill asked Tara, "Do you need your easel?" He caught Tara in mid-yawn.

"Tomorrow," she said. "I made a few sketches today. Tomorrow I'll try to paint."

Bill and Russ exchanged knowing glances. "I don't know what all of you want to do," Bill said, "but I'm going to hit the sack. If anyone wants to stay up, I'll leave this water to put out the fire."

Though the sun had barely slipped behind the mountains, none of the campers felt like lingering by the fire. Walking a bit stiffly, they headed for their tents.

During the night, it wasn't marauding grizzly bears that made Jessa miserable. Three times she had to creep out of her tent to use the primitive privy. The third time she crawled back into the tent and zipped up the flap behind her, Melanie sat up with a start, waving her arms around.

"Shoo!" she said. "Bill? Help!"

"It's just me," Jessa whispered.

"Who's that?" Melanie still sounded panicky.

"Me, Jessa. Sorry—I had to go to the bathroom."

Melanie lay back down. Her cot squeaked as she shifted around, trying to find a comfortable position. "I thought you were a bear," she muttered.

"Sorry," Jessa said, crawling back into her sleeping bag. The only answer from her roommate was a loud snort which then turned into a steady snore.

Jessa shivered. It sure didn't feel like the beginning of summer. The mountain air was freezing cold. She closed her eyes and found herself thinking about what she would be able to drink at breakfast. She wished she had kept her water bottle in her tent—surely no bear would be interested in plain water?

"That's not bad, ma'am," Russ commented as he looked over Tara's shoulder at her drawing. She had her pad balanced on her knees and her plate full of pancakes and sausages on a flat rock beside her.

"Thank you." She sketched quickly, capturing the shadows and folds of the mountains with broad strokes of her pencil.

"If you can make do with sketching during the day, we can bundle up the easel with the sleeping bags again. This evening you'll have lots of time to set up your paints."

"Great—thanks." Jessa noticed that Tara was beginning to look a little more like someone on a wilderness trip. She wore a thick sweater over her jeans and her hair tumbled loose over her shoulders. She hadn't had time before breakfast to put on any makeup and Jessa thought that if anything, Tara looked even prettier without lipstick and eyeshadow.

"The lunch lookout has a great view back through the pass," Russ said. He turned to look at Jessa, who was draining her third glass of apple juice.

"Can you come and give me a hand with the horses?"

"Sure," Jessa agreed quickly. She wiped her mouth with the back of her hand and dropped her plastic cup into the horse bucket that served double duty as the kitchen sink. Rick and Dianne were the designated dish-washers for the day. Jessa wasn't looking forward to her turn at that messy job. She'd rather help get the horses ready any time.

The camp soon bustled with activity as everyone prepared for another day's ride deeper into the mountains. The destination today was Skoki Lake, where the group would camp for two nights. Another semi-permanent set of tents awaited them up on the high mountain plateau near the lake.

When all the chores were done, the pack horses loaded, and the riding horses saddled, the riders gathered at the rope corral.

There was a lot of groaning as the riders mounted up.

"Just wait until tomorrow," Bill quipped. "Day three is always the worst for city slickers!"

As they fell into line, Jessa took little comfort in the fact that her rump felt fine. The rest of her felt decidedly unwell. A vague, lingering nausea and a nasty headache made her think she was coming down with the flu again. On the other hand, no sooner had she mounted up when she began to feel hungry. She had more or less resigned herself to feeling perpetually parched and had made sure to refill her water bottle before they set off.

Jessa was determined not to let anything interfere with her enjoyment of the day. She concentrated on her surroundings. It wasn't hard to be impressed by the stunning scenery that rolled past like a gorgeous movie.

"Mountain goats!" Russ said, stopping his horse. Up on the side of the mountain Jessa could see small white dots balanced precariously on the face of a steep cliff.

"Do they ever fall off?" Tara marvelled.

It didn't seem like there could be much in the way of footholds on the sheer rock face.

"Not often! They're pretty amazing, aren't they?"

Other creatures kept them company during the ride. Russ pointed out ground squirrels, ravens, a blue grouse, and lots of magpies.

"Won't be long until lunch, Jessa!" Bill called from behind her after a couple of hours in the saddle.

She swivelled around to nod back at him and had to steady herself by grabbing hard onto the saddle horn.

The sun must be hotter than I realized, she thought, turning slowly back towards the front. She was a little dizzy, and her pounding headache was getting worse by the minute. *One more step and one more step*, she chanted to herself under her breath. She didn't want to tell Bill she was really feeling awful. He'd want to take her back to the lodge and that would spoil everyone's trip. Who would cook if Bill had to escort her back down the trail?

Besides, Jessa told herself, *it was probably just the sun*. She tugged the brim of her cowboy hat (which Bing had insisted she take) low over her eyes and wrapped her fingers around the saddle horn. *One more step and one more step* . . . Once they reached the lunch place she could have another drink and then rest for a little while. The wranglers kept saying the second day's ride was easier than the first, even for people who were saddle sore. It should have been a snap for someone like her who spent as many hours in the saddle each week as she possibly could.

"Almost there!" Russ called back to the riders nearly an hour later.

By this time, Jessa was hanging onto the horn for dear life. Her arms ached from the effort of holding on and she felt so weak and dizzy she could barely keep herself upright in the saddle. *Just up over the rise and she could let go. . . she could . . .*

"Jessa!"

From very far away she heard Bill calling to her. *One more step, one more step* echoed in her head like she was in a dream. Her head didn't hurt any more and it seemed like the sun had faded, though Jessa thought this was strange since there hadn't been a cloud in the sky all morning. The sounds around her grew fainter and fainter and she couldn't tell any more if she was riding or floating or falling.

The picnic spot must be very close now, she thought and then everything stopped and Jessa couldn't hear anything at all—not the sound of the horse's feet clattering against the barren, stony ground, not the shouts and calls of the other riders, not the crackle of the emergency radio. For Jessa, there was simply a great, dark, silent nothingness.

Chapter Nine

"Jessa? Sweetheart?"

Something very strange was happening. Jessa could have sworn she heard her mother's voice.

"Hey, pumpkin. Can you open your eyes?"

Open her eyes? She must have fallen asleep. Fallen asleep? Where? Jessa struggled to organize the wisps of sound and thoughts all jumbled in her head.

Where was she? Why couldn't she remember? She tried to open her eyes but nothing happened. *Horses. Spirit. The trail ride. She must be having a dream—did she fall asleep beside the trail? But where was everybody else?*

It was a huge effort to remember. To think. *She was so tired—why did her mother keep trying to wake her up?*

Her mother? Jessa struggled to open her eyes. Her mother most certainly had not been on the trail ride but her voice sounded so real, so close. And someone was touching her hand. Stroking her. *What kind of dream was this?*

"Jessa? Honey? Can you please try and open your eyes?"

This was crazy! Jessa's eyelids fluttered and a fuzzy form bent close to her face.

"Jessa?"

"Mom?"

Her own voice sounded small and weak and crackly.

"Oh my God! Nurse? Come quickly!"

Nurse? Why was there a nurse in her dream? Was she really talking or was that a part of the dream, too?

"Jessa! Are you awake?"

"What are you doing here? Where am I?" Jessa put her hand to her face. "Where are my glasses?" No wonder she couldn't see properly.

"Jessa? What's your last name, honey?" a woman's voice asked. *Was this nosy person a nurse? And why did she want to know her last name?*

"Richardson, of course. Mom? What's going on?"

"It's okay, honey. Oh thank God, you're going to be okay. She will be okay now, won't she?"

The nurse handed Jessa her glasses and helped her put them on. All at once, Jessa took in a dozen things. First was her mother's face, which was the strangest mix of pure joy and anguish Jessa had ever seen. Tears glistened on her cheeks and she kept reaching towards her daughter but never quite touching her. Sunshine streamed through big windows into a stark white hospital room Jessa seemed to have all to herself. Flowers crowded every surface and the nurse wore a smock decorated with teddy bears.

"You'll be fine, dear. Your mother is just so happy to see you awake!"

"Where are the horses?" Jessa asked, completely bewildered. She lifted her arm towards her mom and discovered it was attached to a tube connected to a bag hanging from a hook above her. Liquid dripped from the bag, down the tube, and into a needle stuck in her arm.

"Be careful, dear. Use your other arm. We had to give you an IV."

"What is going on? Did I get bucked off?"

"Oh, I almost wish you had!" Jessa's mother sat on the side of the bed. The look on her face had turned in a moment from one of joy and relief to sadness and concern.

"I'm going to page the doctor, Mrs. Richardson. He'll want to see Jessa." The nurse hurried out of the hospital room.

"Am I dreaming?" With every passing minute Jessa wished harder and harder that it *was* a dream, that any minute she would wake up beside a mountain stream, climb back on Spirit, and continue on with her trail ride.

But her mother shook her head. She squeezed Jessa's hand tightly and then leaned forward and kissed her daughter on the forehead. "Oh, Jessa, I can't tell you how good it is to see you awake again. You've been in a coma for hours. I was lucky to get a flight."

Jessa stared at her mother blankly. She couldn't remember being in a coma. *What was her mother talking about?*

"A coma? Why?"

Vaguely, Jessa remembered people sometimes went into comas when they'd been in bad car accidents and hit their heads. "Did I fall off and hit my head?"

"No. You were very lucky. Bill said you were all slowing down for lunch and he saw you starting to slump over. He said he's never jumped off a horse so fast in his life! He broke your fall as you were sliding off your horse. He's been so worried—he keeps calling."

Jessa remembered the sun, the heat, and her headache. "Did I get sunstroke?"

Again, her mother shook her head and squeezed her hand more tightly. "I'm afraid not. I . . . you . . ."

"Mrs. Richardson! I heard the great news! Sleeping Beauty has woken up! Hello, Jessa! The name is Dr. Millowski. How are you feeling?"

Jessa stared at him blankly. *How was she feeling? Was he kidding?*

"Fine." It wasn't exactly a snappy comeback, but Jessa was still feeling too groggy to think straight.

"Good! It's great to finally meet you properly! You've been a pretty boring guest so far! Let me listen to your chest a moment, may I?"

"What's wrong with me? What am I doing here?"

"Hold on a second . . . there. Your heart sounds fine."

"Is there something wrong with my heart?" Jessa wondered for a minute if she'd had a heart attack. She couldn't remember any chest pains.

"No, Jessa, your ticker is just fine. But I'm afraid your pancreas has stopped producing insulin. Do you know what your pancreas does?"

Pancreas? Jessa wasn't sure what a pancreas was. She shook her head.

"Your pancreas helps your body use glucose. Your body gets glucose from the food you eat."

Though the doctor spoke slowly and clearly, Jessa couldn't seem to understand what he was saying.

"When a person's pancreas stops making insulin, you have a condition called diabetes."

Dr. Millowski paused and Jessa let this information sink in. *Diabetes?* She knew a little about diabetes and what she knew wasn't good.

"Don't diabetics need to have shots all the time?" It was the only thing she could remember about it.

Dr. Millowski nodded. Jessa looked at her mother, who said nothing, but covered her mouth with her hand, like someone might do at a funeral. The room seemed suddenly chilly and Jessa shuddered.

"It sounds worse than it is. You'll have to stay in the hospital while we teach you about giving yourself injections, testing your blood sugar, and planning your new diet."

"Diet?" Jessa had never been on a diet in her life. She remembered something else she had heard about diabetics. "Does this mean I can never eat anything sweet again? No more ice cream?"

"It's not healthy for anyone to eat too much cake and candy. You can still have sweets and ice cream sometimes. You just sometimes need to have these foods as part of a meal or snack."

Jessa rested her head back on the pillow and closed her eyes. *This couldn't be happening to her. It just wasn't possible. Shots? Special food? Blood tests?* She bit her lower lip. *Maybe if she kept her eyes closed for long enough she would wake up and find out that none of this was really happening.* She kept her eyes shut even when Dr. Millowski reassured her that everything would be okay and didn't open them when she heard her mother leave the room with him. She heard them mumble together outside her hospital room door and a few minutes later, listened to her mother sinking into the chair at her bedside.

Her mother took her hand and Jessa squeezed it tightly. But she didn't open her eyes again for a long time.

Chapter Ten

"Hi there, Jessa!"

"Hi, Alice!" Jessa liked the freckled young nurse who hummed wherever she went.

"Would you like to try a finger poke yourself?"

Jessa cringed. She had been awake for two days and was only just beginning to understand how different her life would be as a person with diabetes. The only good thing so far was that at least she knew what was wrong with her and that she wasn't likely to die because of her condition. Practically, though, the fact she was no longer constantly thirsty or checking around for the closest bathroom was the biggest relief.

"I'm scared." Jessa didn't want to make a mistake when she did a blood test on her own.

"I know, pet. Believe it or not, you will get used to this."

Everybody kept telling her that, but it seemed impossible she would ever get used to having shots morning and night and blood tests four times a day.

"Could you please do it?"

Alice nodded. "Wipe your finger." Jessa took the warm face cloth and cleaned her finger. She held out her hand to Alice and scrunched up her face.

"I haven't done anything yet! Don't look so horrified!"

"It hurts!"

Alice clicked the grey blood-letting device and took Jessa's hand. She pressed the end of the pen-like stabber against the tip of Jessa's finger and pressed a little button. Jessa jumped, in surprise as much as from the pain.

"That wasn't so bad, was it?" Alice asked. She squeezed Jessa's finger until a bright red drop of blood welled up on her fingertip. The red drop hung over the test strip that stuck out of the blood testing machine. Alice squeezed the drop onto the test strip and the little machine began to count down. Already, the sting of the test had subsided. *It wasn't the worst thing she had ever experienced, but it was bad enough*, Jessa thought.

After thirty seconds, Jessa and Alice both leaned over to read the number showing on the small screen.

"14.2. That's a bit high but not as high as when you first came in. We'll give you some extra insulin before dinner. How are you feeling?"

"Pretty good, actually." How Jessa felt these days seemed to change constantly, depending on what her blood sugar numbers were. When they were high, she had to go to the bathroom and she got hungry and thirsty. When they were low, she felt dizzy and cranky. It was hard to believe that when she had first arrived, her blood sugar reading was 44! Normal people, she learned, don't have readings higher than about 7.0 millimols per litre or lower than 4.0.

Jessa's challenge was to try to keep her blood sugar level as close to normal as possible by using insulin and being careful about when and what she ate. Dr. Millowski and the nurses kept reassuring her that once they had figured out what her insulin doses should be, she would feel pretty good most of the time. This didn't sound promising to Jessa. She wanted to feel great *all* of the time.

"Jessa?"

"Hi, Mom."

"You have a special visitor!"

Jessa wondered who on earth would come to see her in Calgary. She couldn't believe her bad luck that not only was she sick, she was sick in a city where nobody knew her. If she were in Victoria, at least all her friends could come to visit her.

Her mother stepped aside and a tall, bony man stepped into the room. His sandy hair was speckled with grey and he clutched nervously at a large, black teddy bear.

Jessa gasped.

"Dad?!" Mike Richardson was the last person on the planet she had expected to see.

Her father didn't say anything. He sat on her bed, leaned forward and gave her a scratchy kiss on the cheek.

"Sorry—I couldn't shave on the plane!"

"Dad! I can't believe you came!" Jessa heard the uneasy edge in her own voice, as well as her father's.

"It was about time for another visit." He handed Jessa the bear and punched her gently in the shoulder. "You sure gave everyone a scare, miss! Falling off a horse in a coma. Could you have been more dramatic?" He was trying to joke with her, but his worry was obvious.

Jessa's mother tried to lighten the tone. "Did you know they had to fly her here in a helicopter?"

Jessa followed her mother's lead. "The chopper had to land up in the valley. I wish I'd been awake—that would have been so cool!"

"You know, there are other ways to organize a helicopter ride other than being deathly ill!" Her father seemed a bit more relaxed.

"Are you here alone?" It suddenly occurred to Jessa that her father might have brought along his new wife and baby.

"I came alone. It's a long way to travel from Japan, especially for someone as young as Kiri. I thought . . ." He stared hard at the vase of flowers on Jessa's bedside table. Jessa's mother cleared her throat loudly. "I'm glad to see you're okay," he said quickly.

Jessa's father had lived in Japan for years. He almost never came to visit. It was a strange feeling to realize how serious her illness really was. He wouldn't have come, otherwise.

The last time they had seen each other was during the Christmas holidays in Kenwood when a big blizzard had snowed in the whole family. Jessa kept hoping that one day she would be able to visit her father and his new family, but so far, that hadn't happened. She wondered whether it ever would, now that she had diabetes.

"You look so sad, pumpkin!"

Jessa shrugged. "Dad . . . I . . ."

"Shhhhh, don't cry. You'll be okay."

Every day, it seemed like fifty people insisted she would be okay. *But how could that be true when her life was completely ruined? How would she test her blood at school? How could she ever go on a trail ride? What if she fainted because she had low blood sugar? How could she ever travel anywhere?* At that moment, Jessa's life seemed hopeless. There was nothing she could do to stop the sobs that shook her body. She leaned into her father's shoulder and felt his arms around her.

"Shhhhh, Jessa," he said, patting her back. "Everything will be okay. You'll see."

"When are you leaving?" Jessa knew her question wasn't fair, but she was suddenly furious with her father. How dare he show up just because she had nearly died? Obviously, she wasn't worth the trouble when she was healthy.

"I've booked ten days off work."

That was a long time for her father to be away. He rarely took holidays and certainly didn't make a habit of "wasting" them on Jessa. His last visit was really an afterthought—a detour on his way back from business meetings in California. He would have stayed only a few days if the blizzard hadn't interfered with his travel plans.

"When I called the hospital, they said that's how long it would take for me to learn how to look after you."

"Why would you have to learn how to look after me? You're never around," Jessa said bitterly. She pulled away and stuffed the teddy bear at the back of the bedside table, behind the vase of flowers.

"I don't know if we should be talking about . . ."

"Go ahead," Jessa's mother said coolly. "Jessa's not a baby any more."

Jessa's father paused, trying to find the right words. "There are two reasons," he said finally. "If anything ever happened to your mother—" The look of horror on Jessa's face stopped him mid-sentence.

"Not that anything's going to happen! But you know how grown-ups are. We worry."

Jessa's mother jumped in. "Actually, before you got sick, your father and I were discussing something on e-mail. . . ."

"I'd really like for you to come and visit me in Japan," he finished. "That's my second reason. But, it can't happen unless I learn something about your diabetes."

"Really?" Jessa was stunned. *A visit to Japan? That's why he had come?* She glanced over at the bear she had shoved aside and felt a stab of guilt—but then, something else occurred to her. If her parents were discussing travel plans, why hadn't they consulted her before now?

Jessa slumped back against the pillow. *A trip to Japan?*

She would believe it when it happened.

"Okay, now show me what your breakfast might look like."

Brian pushed the basket of plastic food towards Jessa. She didn't mind the lessons with the nutritionist. He made lots of jokes and never tried to poke her with anything.

She rooted around in the basket and fished out a fried egg and two slices of toast.

"Looks good enough to eat!" laughed Brian when Jessa arranged the fake food on a plate. From a tray, Jessa selected a glass that had been painted white. That was supposed to represent a glass of milk.

"Brian, what happens when Jessa and I are running late in the morning? I don't have time to cook breakfasts every day. . . ."

Jessa wished her mother would just observe the lesson and not ask so many questions. It was embarrassing to have her interfering constantly, especially since every time she spoke, the edge of worry in her voice was unmistakable.

"That's easy, Mom." Jessa tipped the egg and toast back in the basket. Jessa glanced over at her father, who sat quietly by her mother. He, too, looked concerned, but at least he didn't constantly jump in with questions.

"I could have this instead," Jessa said, holding up a plastic bagel.

"What about some protein?" Brian asked.

"I was just getting to that. I'd have some peanut butter on it and drink my milk in the car."

"Excellent!" Brian didn't say anything about their being so disorganized in the mornings that sometimes Jessa had to eat breakfast in the car. Now it was time for her mother to look a little embarrassed. "Okay, how about morning snack?"

One of the strangest things about her new meal plan was that Jessa had to eat the right amount of food at set times. This meant she needed snacks in the middle of the morning, in the afternoon, as well as at bedtime.

"Are you sure my teachers will let me eat in the classroom?"

"Absolutely. They have to or you could get dizzy and confused or even faint! You certainly wouldn't be able to concentrate very well."

That was a grim thought. School was hard enough when she could think straight.

"You and your mother will have to talk to your teachers, explain the new routine, and give them this pamphlet. Thousands of kids in Canada have diabetes. Many of them have snacks in the classroom. And, if you go low, you'll need to eat some glucose tabs or drink juice right away. Pretty soon all this will seem totally normal."

Jessa doubted that.

"I'll bet some of your friends might be jealous."

That Jessa could believe. Cheryl would no doubt love to snack in the middle of math class.

"Jessa?" Cathy, one of several teaching nurses who worked at the hospital, poked her head into the nutritionist's office. "Ah, here you are. Can I steal her from you, Brian? We're doing the insulin lesson this morning and I have patients booked for the rest of the day."

"No problem. We can do some more work tomorrow."

Jessa nodded. Far from being restful, life in the hospital was a continuous stream of lessons, reading assignments, and discussions with doctors and nurses. The young interns just learning about kids and diabetes asked more questions than Jessa's mother. Dutifully, she and her parents followed the nurse down the hallway to another office.

None of them were looking forward to this lesson. But before Jessa could leave the hospital, everyone had to learn how to give her insulin injections.

Just like in the movies, Cathy flicked the syringe, held it up to the light, and squirted a tiny stream of liquid across the office.

"You have to make sure there are no air bubbles. Who knows why?"

"To make sure I get every drop of insulin I need." Jessa felt rather smug. She had been reading her handouts.

"Right. Excellent. Who wants to go first?"

"I guess I will," Jessa's father volunteered. Jessa smiled at him gratefully. He was taking the lessons very seriously, and after the initial shock of his arrival, Jessa was surprised to find she was actually enjoying his company. His goofy sense of humour made it a little easier to deal with her mother's constant worrying. This morning, though, he wasn't cracking many jokes.

Cathy explained the procedure. "We are just going to use saline solution and this sponge ball for practising. When everyone feels comfortable, you can decide who will give Jessa a real injection of insulin at supper tonight."

The syringe quivered in her father's hands. He took the sponge ball from Cathy and looked at her for further instructions.

"Okay, now push the needle into the ball."

Tentatively, he poked the needle in.

"You have to push hard. . . ." He sounded surprised.

"It's a little easier to poke it into a person, but this is good practice. Now, push the plunger slowly and evenly until all the liquid is gone."

"Good. Mom, your turn," Cathy directed.

When all three Richardsons had given the sponge ball an injection, Cathy looked at them all seriously.

"Now, Mom and Dad, you are going to practise giving each other saline injections. Then, Jessa, you can give injections to your parents."

Jessa grinned, especially when she saw her father turn pale.

"Why do *we* have to have injections? I don't like needles!"

"It hardly seems fair that you would practise on poor Jessa! She'll be having more than her share of injections and it's important for you to know what Jessa is experiencing. Now don't be such a wimp!"

Jessa loved it when the nurses scolded her parents.

"So, first draw up the liquid in a clean syringe."

Jessa could see that her mother's hands were shaking, too. It was amazing how nervous her parents seemed to be.

"That's good. Now pinch up a bit of Mike's skin on his arm."

"Ow!"

"Gently! Now, push in the needle, just like you did with the sponge ball."

Jessa's mom hesitated.

"Come on, Mom. Hurry up!"

The tip of the needle disappeared into her father's arm. He pulled a face and looked away.

"Good. Now, push in the plunger and slowly let go of the pinch. Not quite that slowly . . . there, good!"

Jessa's mom pulled out the needle and slipped on the orange cap. Her father rubbed his arm and let out his breath. "That wasn't actually so bad! It didn't really hurt."

"They are very tiny needles. Sometimes, you don't even feel it go in at all."

Jessa looked at the nurse doubtfully. It was amazing how matter-of-fact everybody was, as if giving injections was as normal as brushing teeth.

"Okay, Mr. Richardson, your turn."

It was hard to tell who had to be braver—her mother who had to receive the injection, or her father who had to give it.

"Excellent! Congratulations, both of you! Now, Jessa—your turn to give shots to your parents."

Now that Jessa was the one holding the syringe, she, too, felt nervous. *What if she did it wrong? What if she hurt someone?* "What if the needle breaks off inside his arm?" she asked as she checked for bubbles and eyed her father's arm.

"Could that happen?" he asked, aghast.

"No—the needles are very tough. They can bend, though, so you do have to be careful."

This comment did little to reassure Jessa. It was much harder to poke the needle into her father's arm than it had been to inject the sponge ball.

"Ow!" he said, and she jerked the needle back out.

"Try again, Jessa. It's okay—your dad's a big, tough guy!"

"No, I'm not! Shoot your mother now!"

"Mr. Richardson, cooperate!" Cathy shot Jessa's father a no-nonsense look.

"It's okay, pumpkin. Sorry I jumped like that. You know how I am about needles . . . go ahead, try again."

"I don't want to hurt you!" Jessa voice shook. This was not fun, giving her parents injections.

Cathy coaxed and cajoled and finally, Jessa tried again. This time, the needle slid in smoothly and she had no trouble at all pushing in the plunger. She sat back in her chair and grinned.

"That wasn't so bad," she said.

"Easy for you to say," her dad groaned, clutching his arm. "I'm kidding," he said quickly, seeing the look of concern on her face. "Sorry, that was a bad joke—it really didn't hurt at all that time!"

"Remember, you have to rotate your injection sites. What does that mean, Jessa?"

Being in hospital was as bad as being at school. "I can use my arms, legs, and stomach, and I have to keep changing where I inject so one spot doesn't get sore."

When the three of them were finished their shot-giving lesson, they fled from Cathy's office.

"Anybody else want to go for a walk?" Jessa's dad asked.

"Yes, please!" Jessa's mother sounded very enthusiastic about getting out of the hospital for a while. "Oh, wait. What do we need to bring? Insulin?"

"No, I don't get another shot until supper time. But we should take a juice box and some glucose tablets in case I go low."

"Low? Will you know if you are going low?" Her mother sighed. "How are we ever going to cope when we leave here?"

Jessa shook her head. At that moment it all seemed so overwhelming, she couldn't imagine ever going home.

"We'll stick close to the hospital," her dad said. "We'll just walk around in the gardens in case . . ." His voice trailed off. There were so many "in cases" to worry about.

A lump rose in Jessa's throat. *This was crazy. She couldn't even just go for a walk any more without having to think about taking juice and glucose tablets. She hated diabetes more than she had ever hated anything in her life.*

Chapter Eleven

"Mail call!" Alice dropped a stack of letters on Jessa's bed. "I don't know where you're going to put them!"

All the folks from Flannigan's had sent cards and flowers and Bill had sent a giant poster of a bronc rider. Jessa had given the poster a place of honour on the wall at the foot of the bed.

"Look, here's one from Cheryl!"

Jessa tore open the bright orange envelope from her best friend. In typically outrageous Cheryl form, her friend had stuffed the envelope full of goodies. Stickers, several bookmarks, and a large piece of paper folded in half and half again made the envelope bulge.

"Oh my," Jessa's father said when she unfolded the poster her friend had made. It was a very dramatic picture of helicopter with a big red cross painted on its side.

In bright green letters painted over the sky, Cheryl had written GET WELL SOON! All around the edge of the poster, making a kind of frame, she had drawn about fifty syringes end to end, complete with bright orange caps. They looked very authentic. Jessa was impressed. Cheryl must have done some research.

Her handmade card was also cheerful. She had drawn a picture of Rebel on the card and inside wrote:

Hi Jessa! How are you doing? I hope you don't have to stay in the hospital for much longer because it is boring around here without you. Anthony has a friend who has diabetes and they were telling me all about the shots and everything. Ouch! Can I watch when you give yourself shots?

I went to the library and took out four books about diabetes. The diet and the shots and the blood testing are really interesting, don't you think?

Jessa groaned. That was all she needed—for Cheryl to become an overnight medical expert.

I have been to the barn a couple of times because Mrs. Bailey called me and asked if I could keep exercising Billy Jack. You know, the more time I spend with that old horse, the more I like him.

Heeeeeeeelp . . . I'm running out of room so I'd better go. Get your butt home soon! Love, Cheryl.

Jessa had to turn the card sideways and upside down to read the end of Cheryl's message. She wondered how Rebel was doing and noticed that Cheryl hadn't mentioned either her pony or Molly.

"Can I hang the picture on the back of the door?" Jessa asked, not wanting to think about Dark Creek and the way she was wasting precious riding time being in the hospital.

"I'm way ahead of you—here's some tape." Alice pulled a roll of tape from her uniform pocket. "I have to get back to the nurse's station—I'll be back in a while for another blood test."

"Hey! This one's from Jeremy! How did he know where I am?"

"Ooooh," her mother teased. "What does he say?"

Jessa shook her head and read silently.

Hi, Jessa!
I heard about what happened. When will you be

coming back? I'll be away next week because Mom and I are going to a horse show in Vancouver. Rachel was planning to go, but then she changed her mind so she could go to that dressage clinic with Gunther Kubek at Arbutus Lane. I agree her flatwork needs a little help.

Jessa grinned and read quickly through the rest of Jeremy's letter. It was filled with news of the horses his mother was training and the work he was doing with his own horse, Caspian. When she finished reading, she slid the letter into the drawer of her bedside table so she could read it again later—more slowly.

Mrs. Bailey's handwriting scrawled over the next envelope.

Dear Jessa,

I hope you are feeling better. Walter and I have been very worried about you. I hear your father has come to visit. I'm afraid this is just a month for sickness and accidents. I did a very silly thing last week when I was chasing Eric. That cheeky cat was up on the table licking Walter's piece of cheesecake! I rushed towards him to frighten him off and slipped on the loose rug in the kitchen!

Walter, hopeless man, stood in the kitchen door and laughed at me! I was not impressed. Luckily, I didn't break anything, but since I landed on my *behind, I badly bruised my tailbone.*

"Ouch!" Jessa said sympathetically.

I took two days off and then tried to ride Jasmine but I had to get off after a few minutes because it was so painful. My poor baby doesn't know why her mumsy isn't paying attention to her! That boy Jeremy, the one with the black horse, came around looking for you yesterday. I told him what happened. I hope you don't mind.

So, that was how Jeremy had found out where she was.

Marjorie, Betty, Sharon, Molly, and all the horses say hello. Rebel is doing fine but is looking forward to having you back.

Get well soon. Give my regards to your parents.

> *Best Wishes,*
> *Barbara Bailey*

"Any exciting news from the barn?"

"Mrs. Bailey can't ride! She fell on a rug and bruised her backside. That must be driving her crazy!"

"Isn't she getting a bit old to be riding horses?" Jessa's dad asked.

"If you think she's old, you should see her boyfriend! Walter Walters is ancient!"

"Mrs. Bailey has a boyfriend? Really?"

"He's a horse trainer. They don't live together or anything, but Walter comes over for cheesecake a lot. He's a really good rider. He understands horses better than anybody I know."

"I like Walter—he's a good choice for Mrs. Bailey," Jessa's mom added. She liked Mrs. Bailey a lot. "That's too bad about her accident. Do you know how long before she'll be back in the saddle?"

"She doesn't say."

"Have a look at what's in the last one," her father prompted.

Jessa tore open the fat manila envelope and pulled out the contents.

"Wow!" her mother exclaimed when she saw the top drawing. "That's really good!" The package of six drawings was from Tara.

Dear Jessa,

I hope you are feeling better. What a shame you had to miss the rest of the trip—the scenery was spectacular! Rick and I both had a marvellous time. I thought these drawings might cheer you up. By the way, you may be interested to know I never did get a chance to use my easel on the trip, though I am making up for lost time now! Rick and I wish you all the best.

Love, Tara.

The first picture showed the camp by the river. The next was a quick sketch of Bill sitting on a boulder, looking down the valley, his hands wrapped around a steaming mug of coffee. There were a couple of views of the mountains and one of a waterfall. The best drawing was a detailed portrait of Spirit.

"Mom, do you think I could get one of these framed for my room at home?"

"At least you'll have some room at home. It's going to be tough finding space to put all these up here!" Jessa's dad remarked. "I hope you don't get too much more mail before you go home."

"How much longer *do* I have to stay here?"

Jessa's parents exchanged worried looks. Her father cleared his throat. "The doctor says it's normal to stay ten to twelve days after someone wakes up from a coma. It takes that long for you to learn everything you need to know so you and your mother can go home and make sure you stay healthy."

Five red *X*s on a calendar on the wall marked the days she had been at the hospital.

"That means I have to be here another week?" Jessa slumped back on the pillow. "I know enough already. I don't want to stay here. I hate it here!"

"Jessa, honey . . ." Jessa pulled her hand away from her mother's concerned touch.

"Go away! Don't tell me everything is going to be okay! That's what everyone says but it isn't true! Nothing will ever be okay again!"

"Susan . . . why don't we go down to the cafeteria for a little while. Maybe Jessa needs a little time by herself."

"I'll be fine! Go. You can eat whatever you want down there! Enjoy it!"

The words spat out of her mouth. When her parents left the room and closed the door softly behind them, Jessa felt a strange mixture of rage and sadness. She wanted to go with them, but at the same time, she didn't want anybody near her. Jessa drove her head into her pillow and cried. *This isn't fair! Why did this have to happen?*

"Jessa?" Alice tapped on the door. "Jessa, can I come in for a minute? You mom told me you were upset. Do you mind if I take a blood test?"

"Right now? It's not time!" Jessa sniffled.

"I know. But sometimes if you go low, you might feel like crying."

"Fine."

Neither Jessa nor the nurse said a word while Alice quickly pricked Jessa's finger to take a blood sample. After the blood tester had counted down, Alice read the number.

"7.2. That's excellent." Alice packed away her equipment. "I'm sorry to have bothered you."

When the door had closed behind the nurse, Jessa leaned back against the pillow and closed her eyes. The urge to cry had passed and she simply felt defeated. Empty. *This was completely insane. She couldn't even have a good cry when something truly rotten happened to her without people worrying that her blood sugar was low! Now, feeling miserable was a medical emergency!* Despite herself, Jessa had to smile at just how absurd the thought was that she couldn't even have a decent temper tantrum any more.

Chapter Twelve

"That's it! We've just finished the final teaching unit," Cathy smiled at Jessa and her parents. "Jessa, Doctor Millowski is very pleased with your progress. He has called your family doctor back in Victoria . . . Dr. Billings, isn't it? You should go in for a checkup when you get back. Just like here, there's a clinic for children and teens with diabetes at the hospital in Victoria."

The lessons of the previous ten days blurred in Jessa's mind. She had learned about adjusting her insulin dose, what to do when she was sick with the flu and couldn't eat, and how to handle changing blood sugars when she exercised. For the past three days she had been giving herself insulin injections and testing her own blood sugars.

"You've done very, very well, Jessa. You'll be just fine once you get home. If you have any questions, just call the clinic."

Despite the nurse's assurances, now that her time at the hospital was coming to an end, Jessa didn't feel at all sure that she would be fine.

"Couldn't I just stay here for another week?" she asked. "I still don't know everything."

"That's true. But the things you need to learn now you can only learn by going home. We don't have horses here, for one thing. And until you try a few days of riding, you won't know exactly how much extra snack food you'll need, or if you have to adjust your insulin a little on riding days."

"What if I do it wrong?"

Her father spoke up. "It's okay, Jessa. You and your mom will be fine."

It was easy for her father to say everything would be okay. He was leaving on a flight back to Japan later in the afternoon. He didn't have to worry about anything after today.

As if he had read her mind, her father added, "And we'll keep talking on e-mail about having you come to visit me. Okay?"

"Sure. Okay." Jessa was glad he hadn't forgotten about the trip to Japan, but she still wasn't going to believe it would actually happen until the day she held a plane ticket in her hand.

"We'll do our best, Jessa," her mother said. "And if we have any problems, just like Cathy said, we can always call the clinic or Dr. Billings."

"That's right," Cathy said. "So, Jessa, pack up your things—and don't forget your cards and that great poster from your friend!"

There was no time to argue. Cathy hurried out of the room, off to talk with another patient.

Jessa's mother stood up. "Jessa . . . we can't stay here forever. Let me help you pack."

At the airport, Jessa stood awkwardly in front of her father near the international departure gates.

"Bye, Dad. Thanks for coming."

"Why does it seem I only see you when some sort of disaster happens?" Jessa knew he meant it as a joke but she could only manage a small smile.

"Yeah. We have to stop meeting like this."

"We'll see each other again before too long."

Jessa caught the glance that passed between her parents. Travelling so far on her own had been a scary thought *before* diabetes. Now that she knew how much was involved in managing daily life, she had serious doubts she would ever be able to travel anywhere.

"I'll e-mail you, Dad."

"I'll write back. I promise."

Jessa wondered if he really would. Between his busy job in Tokyo and his new family, he didn't have a lot of time. At least, that was the excuse he always used.

"Passengers boarding Flight 1007 to Tokyo, please proceed to gate A-4 in the international departure area. Thank you."

"I guess that's me. Goodbye, Jessa. Let me know how you're doing. Good luck."

He gave her a rough squeeze and then turned and quickly walked away. Feeling her throat tighten, Jessa remembered why she hated airports and how much she really hated it that her father lived so far away.

"Come on, Jessa. Let's go to the cafeteria and wait for our flight. You can do a blood test and then have your afternoon snack." Jessa felt her mother's soft touch on her arm. She turned and buried her face in her mother's shoulder.

"Excuse me, miss. Do you have any diet soda? My daughter is a diabetic. She can't have any pop with sugar in it."

Jessa groaned inwardly. The flight attendant nodded kindly and found a diet drink in her tray. Already her mother had managed to tell about eight thousand people that her daughter was a diabetic. At the cafeteria, she had made the cook weigh the scone Jessa had eaten for her snack, and before they boarded the plane, she had grilled the woman at the ticket counter to find out if there would be unsweetened fruit juices on board.

"Mom, you don't have to tell everybody about it."

"There's nothing to be ashamed of, Jessa. And we have to be careful."

Jessa put on her headphones and cranked up the volume. She tipped her chair back and closed her eyes. About fifteen minutes later, her mother prodded her in the arm.

"Are you okay?" she asked.

"I'm fine. Why?"

"I thought you had fainted."

"Fainted? I just had my eyes closed. I'm listening to the music!"

"Do you think we should do a blood test? Just to make sure you're not going to have an insulin reaction while you're lying there?"

"I would notice if I were going low."

"Not if you're sleeping."

"I'm not sleeping. I'm fine, Mom."

Jessa's mother sighed, her face tense with worry. Jessa had gone low once at the hospital, after a long walk around the hospital grounds. Cathy had said that was a good thing to experience, so Jessa could recognize the signs. When it had happened at the hospital, she had felt dizzy and weak. Right away she had had some juice and two glucose tablets and within a few minutes had started to feel much better.

"I'm fine," she repeated, and closed her eyes again. She was far too old to have her mother hovering over her like that, asking how she was feeling every two minutes. If the diabetes wasn't going to drive her crazy, her mother certainly would.

"Can I call Cheryl?"

"Jessa, it's ten o'clock!"

"It's the summer holidays. And besides, nobody at

Cheryl's house goes to bed early."

It was true. Cheryl's family owned a small theatre company. Since they often worked late at night, they rarely got up early and nearly always stayed up late.

"I have to find out how Romeo is doing."

"Couldn't you wait until tomorrow? I'm sure he's fine."

Jessa's mother looked exhausted.

"Please? I'll be quick."

"Fine. But don't talk for long—you have to go to bed soon."

It was one of the mysteries of adult thinking that just because her mother was tired, she figured Jessa should go to bed early, too.

"Hi, Cheryl?"

"Jeeeessssssaaaaaa! You're back!"

"We just got in. How's Romeo?"

"How's Romeo? You've been away for three weeks lying at death's door and scaring everyone and you get back and ask about your dog? How about, 'How's Cheryl?' Aren't I your best friend?"

Jessa grinned. It was sure good to hear Cheryl's voice again. "Wrong again. Everyone knows dogs are man's best friend. Or, in my case, girl's best friend. Besides, I was nowhere near death's door."

"Fine. Be like that. I'm going to hang up on you!"

"Fine. Be like that!"

Both girls giggled. They often played a silly game where they pretended to be having a terrible fight over nothing.

"Okay, Cheryl. How are you?"

"I'm fine. Don't you want to know about your dog?"

"Oh, shut up, you twerp!"

"Nice way to talk to your best friend. Your dog is fine. He pined away for the first couple of days after your mom left. He wouldn't eat!"

"Ooooohhhh . . . poor Romeo!"

"Don't worry—I sat beside him on the kitchen floor and hand-fed him. It drove Ginger crazy." Ginger was Cheryl's dog.

"You had to hand-feed him?"

"Only for the first two days. Then Ginger had a word with him and explained you'd be back soon and he settled down. After that, he was quite a greedy little pig."

That sounded more like the Romeo Jessa knew.

"Can you come over? I want to see your blood tester."

"Right now?" Jessa peeked into the living room. She could just see her mother's toes poking up over the end of the couch. "I doubt it very much. You know how much travelling takes out of grown-ups. My mom has already passed out on the couch."

"Speaking of passing out, do you remember going into the coma?"

"Of course not. I was in a coma. I don't remember anything."

"So I guess it's a dumb question to ask how you liked the trail ride?"

"The part that I remember was great."

Jessa stopped and paused uneasily. The trail ride had been wonderful. It was so depressing to think that she'd never be allowed to go on another trip like that again. It would just be too risky—her insulin might go bad, or the bottle might get broken; they might not have the right kinds of food; she might go low and fall off the horse; or the cowboys might not want someone on a trip who had to carry around syringes and lancets, the sharp needly things Jessa used to prick her fingers.

"I wish I'd taken more photographs," was all she could think of to say.

"Guess what?" Cheryl said quickly.

"What?"

If Jessa could have crawled through the phone to give

her friend a hug, she would have. Cheryl always seemed to know when to change the subject and how to cheer Jessa up.

"I'm going to ride Billy Jack three times a week! Regularly! Sharon says she really likes the way I ride her horse and she said she won't have time this summer to come out more than once or twice a week."

"Really?" Billy Jack was the ugliest horse Jessa had ever met. He had big ears like a mule, wasn't light enough to be white, or yellow enough to be a palomino, so he mostly looked sort of grubby. Jessa wasn't sure how old he was, but judging by the amount of time he needed to warm up to work the stiffness out of his joints, he wasn't exactly a spring chicken.

"Sharon was so happy when I agreed to help keep him in shape."

"That's great! Now we can both ride on trails and stuff."

"That's what I was thinking. Except . . ."

"Except what?"

"Jessa? Are you still on the phone?" Her mother's voice sounded groggy, as if she had half fallen asleep.

"Just a minute, Mom. I'm talking to Cheryl!"

"It's getting late, Jessa. You have to go to bed."

"Okay, okay. What's going on, Cheryl?"

"Nothing. Do you have to go?"

Jessa made a disgusted noise deep in the back of her throat.

"What time can I come to your house tomorrow? I miss Romeo!"

"Not too early. I need my beauty sleep. Not before ten, okay?"

"Fine. I'll see you tomorrow."

"Jessa! Jessa, quickly, wake up!"

"What?" Jessa rubbed her eyes and sat up in bed. It

was so great to be surrounded by all her things again. "What's the matter?"

"You have to get up! We both slept in!"

Jessa sat up in her bed. Her attic room looked just the same as always—horse posters covered the walls and the ceiling and all her shelves were filled with horse books, collectible model horses, and even a couple of small trophies. The back of her door was covered with shiny ribbons of every possible colour that she had won riding Rebel.

The only thing that was different this morning was Jessa. With a rush, she remembered she was a diabetic. Jessa couldn't just run downstairs and have a piece of toast. First she had to test her blood and have a shot. She lay back down on the pillow and closed her eyes again.

"Jessa!" Her mother's voice was insistent. Worried. "You can't go to sleep. You have to get up right now."

"What time is it?"

"Nearly eleven!" Her mother sounded horrified. "Eleven!"

This time, Jessa sat bolt upright and swung her legs over the side of the bed. "Eleven?" she asked in horror. *It couldn't be. She hadn't been that tired!*

"I'm not sure what to do. If you have your normal mix of the two kinds of insulin, the long-lasting stuff won't be working until far too late in the day! You've already missed your breakfast time *and* your morning snack!"

Jessa tried to think what they were supposed to do. She couldn't remember a lesson about sleeping in.

"See, we weren't ready to leave the hospital," Jessa said.

"We can figure this out."

"No, we can't. We can't just change the intermediate-acting dose."

93

Jessa struggled to think through her groggy confusion. The insulin was so complicated. They had to mix two kinds together in one syringe. The short-acting variety started to work very quickly whereas the intermediate-acting stuff kept on working for up to twelve hours.

They sat side by side on the bed. "You're right, I don't think we can do that. First things first. Come downstairs and test your blood sugar. While you're doing that, I'm going to call the hospital." Her mother sounded determined.

"Call the hospital? You mean now sleeping in is a medical emergency?"

"Don't be cheeky. I'll just ask the doctor on call what we should do."

At the kitchen table, Jessa ran through the procedure of pricking her finger and testing her blood. She wrote the number down on a piece of paper and handed it to her mother, who had started talking to the doctor on the phone.

"This is the silliest problem," her mother said apologetically. "My daughter has diabetes—she was only diagnosed a couple of weeks ago and this is our first day at home and something terrible happened. . . ."

At the other end of the phone, the doctor seemed to be saying something reassuring. When her mother went on, she sounded a little calmer. "Well, we must have been very tired from our trip home from Calgary because we both slept in this morning and now I don't know how much insulin to give her."

Jessa rolled her eyes. This was more than a little embarrassing.

"Yes, yes, I have her number right here. She's 16.8." Jessa's mother rattled off the normal amounts of insulin Jessa would normally get as well as her mealtimes and the amounts of food she would usually eat at each.

"So, no intermediate-acting insulin at all?"

They talked for a few more minutes and then her mother hung up and sat down beside Jessa at the table.

"Well, we couldn't have guessed how to do this. Instead of mixing short- and intermediate-acting insulins this morning, you'll just have a shot of short-acting insulin before every meal. He said you should try to eat about every four hours and then by tonight we can go back to our normal routine."

"Isn't this strange?" Jessa asked.

"What do you mean?"

"Well, two weeks ago, your whole conversation on the phone would have sounded like you were talking in a foreign language. We didn't know anything about intermediate-acting, or short-acting, or blood glucose levels, or anything."

Jessa's mother nodded grimly. "I must admit, I wish I still didn't know anything about it."

As Jessa drew up her shot and gave herself an injection in her thigh, she had to agree with her mother. Her mother shook her head and sighed. Jessa knew exactly how she felt.

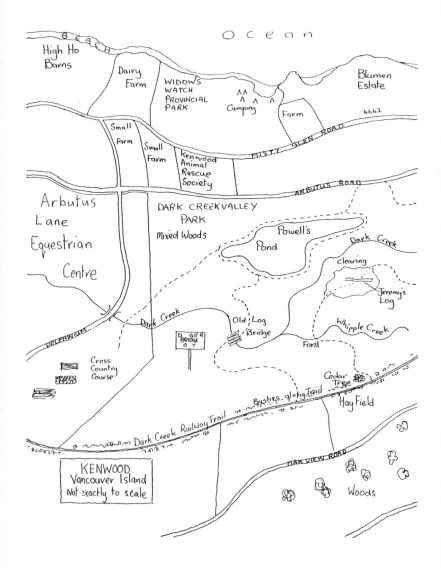

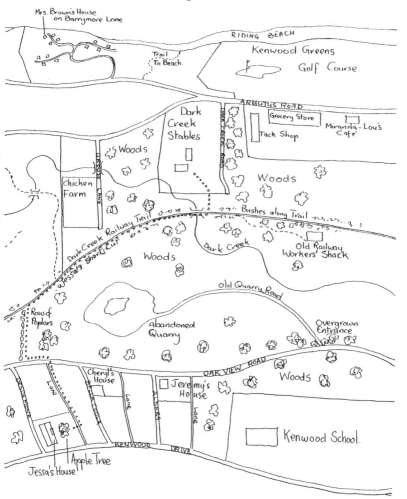

Ocean

Mrs. Brown's House
on Barrymore Lane

RIDING BEACH

Kenwood Greens
Golf Course

Trail
To Beach

ARBUTUS ROAD

Dark
Creek
Stables

Grocery Store

Miranda-Lou's
Café

Tack Shop

Woods

Woods

Chicken
Farm

Dark Creek Railway Trail

Bushes along Trail

Jessa's Short Cut

Woods

Dark Creek

Old Railway
Workers' Shack

Old Quarry Road

Row of
Poplars

Abandoned
Quarry

Overgrown
Entrance

OAK VIEW ROAD

Cheryl's
House

Woods

Jeremy's
House

Lane

Lane

Lane

Kenwood School.

KENWOOD   DRIVE

Apple Tree

Jessa's House

97

Chapter Thirteen

Jessa was nearly finished her breakfast of waffles and eggs when the phone rang.

"Are you coming over, or what?"

"Sorry, Cheryl. We had a little problem over here this morning. We slept in."

"That's a problem?"

"My mom even had to call the hospital."

"Really?" Cheryl sounded impressed. "Are you okay? You're talking funny."

"That'sh becaush my mouf ish full of wafflsh."

"Oh. Good. You shouldn't speak with your mouth full. You sound disgusting. Can you hold the phone away from your mouth so I don't have to listen to you slurping?"

Jessa swallowed. "I'm done. Can I come and get Romeo?"

"Sure. Can you come soon? I'm going to the barn right after lunch. Do you want to come?"

Jessa hesitated and then shook her head. "No. Not today." She didn't like the idea of having to keep track of the weird extra shots she had to take all day because of sleeping in. It was bad enough that she'd have to have extra snacks at the barn on days when she went riding.

Cheryl didn't ask questions. "Okay. I'm ready and waiting for you."

Romeo recognized the rattling noises of the

Richardson's old car when they were still a block away.

"You should have seen him!" Cheryl said. "He started hopping up and down and wiggling! He knew you were coming!"

Romeo slathered Jessa with sloppy dog kisses. "Stop! Good boy!"

"Good thing you spent all that time at obedience classes with that dog!" her mother joked.

"He's so cute!" gushed Cheryl. She pushed her tousled red hair out of her eyes. "Look what I taught him!"

She ran over to the fence and retrieved a hula hoop.

"Romeo! Pay attention!" Cheryl demanded.

Romeo had no interest whatsoever in what Cheryl was doing. He kept licking Jessa, his tail thrashing back and forth with wild glee.

"Romeo!" Cheryl wouldn't give up, despite the fact Jessa had collapsed in helpless giggles. She stood over the naughty dog with her hands sternly jammed on her hips. "Where are your manners? Don't forget who's been feeding you for the past two weeks!"

"Romeo, sit." Jessa managed to gasp. The dog whined and licked his lips, but did as he was told.

"Good dog," said Cheryl, moving until she was standing in front of him with the big hoop. "Stand back out of the way." Cheryl was in her element, preparing to do some fancy trick.

Jessa took a step back, ready for anything.

"Watch this! Romeo the wonder-dog will now perform the most amazing hoop-leap! Romeo—jump!"

Romeo bolted forward, squirmed underneath the hoop, and then raced back to Jessa. He jumped up and put his paws on her chest, still wagging his tail vigorously.

"Oh, very good, Cheryl! You are sure some amazing dog trainer."

"I swear he did it lots of times yesterday!" Cheryl sounded very hurt. "Really, he did! He was going to be the star of my circus act!"

"You'll just have to use your own dog. Sorry! Good boy, Romeo!" Jessa rubbed her dog behind his ears. "Thanks for looking after him for me."

"No problem. It was fun. He's clearly distracted now. You distracted him. When I come over to your house, I'll bring the hoop and I'll show you. He can do it perfectly! He runs right up to it and jumps right through!"

"Sure, Cheryl. I believe you!"

"Who's that?" Jessa asked as she and her mother drove back down Desdemona Street. Romeo's head hung out the back window and he snuffled happily in the breeze.

Somebody was sitting on their front steps. Whoever it was looked up and waved when they heard the rattle and squeak of the Richardson Wreck.

"Granny!"

Jessa ran up the front steps and threw her arms around her grandmother.

"Hello, sweetheart! How are you feeling?"

"Great!"

"Hi, Mabel. How good to see you." The two women hugged on the front steps.

"Susan, how are *you* feeling?"

"Much better after a good night's sleep! I didn't think you were arriving until this evening."

"Better early than . . ." Granny couldn't think of an appropriate saying. "Never mind . . . here I am! Aren't you going to invite me in?"

"Help Granny with her bags, Jessa."

"Romeo! Stop sniffing!" They made their way into the house. Jessa's mother bustled about in the kitchen while Jessa and Granny sat at the kitchen table.

"Oh, Jessa—it's very good to see you again. I'm so sorry your trip didn't quite work out as planned. Here— I brought you something."

"What is it?"

Granny rummaged around in her big handbag and pulled out a small package.

"Open it and see."

Carefully, Jessa peeled back the wrapping paper. Inside were two bars of chocolate. Her face fell. "Granny . . . thank you, but I . . ."

How could her grandmother not have known that diabetics can't just eat candy bars whenever they want?

"Turn over the bar and read the label."

"Hey!" Jessa exclaimed.

"What have you found, Mabel?" Jessa's mother took one of the bars from Jessa. "Appropriate for carbohydrate-reduced diets," she read.

"Now, I asked the pharmacist about these, and he says it's fine for people with diabetes to have two or three squares at a time. But, he said to be careful and work it into your meal plan."

"I wonder what they taste like?"

Jessa felt sure that any kind of fake chocolate probably tasted awful.

"There's only one way to find out. I bought one with nuts and one without because I didn't know which you'd prefer."

Jessa took her steaming mug of tea and peeled back the chocolate bar's silver paper. She broke off a piece and popped it on her tongue. She held it there and waited for the chocolate to start melting.

"Hey," she nodded. "This is pretty good!"

Granny looked relieved. "Good. Now I know what I can send you for a little extra present at Christmas!"

The chocolate bar didn't taste exactly like regular

chocolate, but it was actually very good. Smooth. Chocolatey. "This is really good!" she said, reaching for another piece.

"Remember—only two or three pieces at a time."

"Okay." It was going to be hard to remember not to eat a whole bar in one go.

"The dietition told us there were lots of sugar-free foods we can buy for Jessa—popsicles, pudding, hot chocolate . . . we have to go shopping and re-stock our shelves. And," her mother added, looking tired, "I have to go through the recipe book they gave us to find some healthy meals which have all the proper choices."

"Choices?"

"Well, portions. Jessa has to have certain amounts of each food group at each meal."

Jessa cleared her throat. She hated it when people talked about her like she wasn't there.

"I have a chart that shows what I have to eat."

"It sounds complicated. You know, I can help with the shopping and the cooking. That's why I'm here—to be helpful."

"I know. I'm so glad you came, Mabel."

"You have to go back to work tomorrow, right?"

Now Jessa understood why Granny had come to stay.

"Hey, I don't need a babysitter!"

"Jessa, please! Don't be rude."

"It's fine if Granny wants to come for a visit, but I don't need looking after."

"Jessa! Up to your room. Having diabetes does not mean you can be rude."

"Don't you want to test my blood to make sure I'm not low?"

The words came out of her mouth much more fiercely than she had intended.

"Go. Now!"

As she made her way up the stairs to her room, she

heard her mother's voice saying softly, "I'm sorry, Mabel. She's very upset."

"Don't worry, dear. I understand. Of course she's upset. So am I! So are you . . ."

Jessa flopped down on her bed and stared at the giant poster stuck to her ceiling. The prancing horse looked like it was going to dance right down on top of her. But the only thing that landed on her was Romeo, who seemed to sense her unhappiness and whined as he licked her face.

She scrunched her eyes shut and sighed. *Why had she said those things? She didn't even mean them!* It was a very good thing her grandmother had come to stay. The last thing Jessa wanted was to be left alone all day while her mother went to work.

Jessa patted Romeo, rolled off the bed, and went to her desk. She took out a piece of her horse-head writing paper.

Dear Granny, I'm sorry I behaved like a jerk. I am glad you are here. Thank you for the chocolate. Maybe we can go to . . .

She stopped writing. Whenever her grandmother had come to Victoria on day trips before, the two of them had often visited the little petting zoo at Beacon Hill Park. After that, they usually fed the ducks and then went to the Beacon Hill Drive-in for a soft ice cream cone. Well, *that* wasn't going to happen any more. Not unless they carefully scheduled their visit to coincide with mealtimes or if she conveniently went low right when they arrived at the ice cream stand. As far as Jessa could see, there would be no more spur-of-the-moment ice cream in her future.

She scrawled a picture of an ice cream cone at the bottom of the sheet of paper and then scratched a heavy, dark X right through it. Then Jessa crumpled the letter in a ball and threw it at her closed door as hard as she could.

Chapter Fourteen

"Jessa?"

The clock radio said 2:30 p.m. There was another knock at the door.

"Come in, Granny."

Jessa put her horse magazine on the stack she had piled on the bed. Before her grandmother had a chance to say anything, Jessa apologized.

"I don't know why I said that stuff."

Granny shook her head. "Not to worry. Apology accepted. Your mother tells me it's lunchtime for you."

The smell of grilled cheese sandwiches drifted up the stairs into Jessa's room.

"Yum! I'm getting hungry."

"Listen, I was wondering if, after lunch, we could go down to the barn so I can see your pony. I haven't seen Rebel for ages."

"I don't know, Granny. I really don't feel like—"

"Now, Jessa. If we go right after lunch we'll have a few hours before you have to eat again. I'm sure we can manage even with today's strange schedule. Your mother told me what happened, but you can't stop living your life just because things don't always go smoothly. Don't you want to see Rebel?"

Jessa nodded reluctantly. It would be nice to see her pony again and at least he wouldn't constantly ask her if she felt okay.

Granny didn't give Jessa a chance to back out.

"Great. Come on downstairs—your mother is waiting with hot grilled cheese sandwiches."

"Come on, Romeo," Jessa said. "Grilled cheese is your favourite, isn't it, boy?"

Jessa grinned cheekily at her grandmother's disapproving face.

"You shouldn't feed that dog at the table. You'll spoil him."

"I think it's too late for that, Granny!"

"Disgusting, is what it is. That's how you train a dog to beg!"

"Come on, Granny. Let's go eat. I'll be discreet. I'll drop the crusts under the table where you won't be able to see!"

"Oh, Jessa!"

"Oh, no!"

"What's the matter, Jessa?" Granny asked.

"Look!"

"That looks a lot like your pony."

"It *is* my pony! That girl is riding him again!"

"Didn't you call Mrs. Bailey to say you were coming?"

"No." Jessa had never needed to call before. Rebel was supposed to be her pony. It wasn't right that she had to call ahead to make arrangements to ride him.

"Jessa! Hello!" Mrs. Bailey trotted over to the fence at the side of the riding ring. "Take a break, Molly! That's a girl."

"I didn't know you were coming down today or we could have scheduled Molly's lesson for another day. I am sorry! How are you feeling, dear?"

Mrs. Bailey tipped her big black cowboy hat back out of her eyes and looked Jessa over carefully. "I must say you look a tad better than the last time I saw you. I knew something strange was going on when you couldn't lift those hay bales!"

Jessa could hardly force herself to speak civilly. "Does she ride him every day?"

"No, dear. Only three or four times a week. You owe her a big thank you for keeping Rebel in good shape while you were away."

Jessa bit the inside of her cheek. *A big thank you? Ha! Maybe a big punch in the nose for horse-stealing.*

"We're just finishing off our lesson. Why don't you stay and watch and then you could take Rebel out on a trail ride to cool him out. You don't even have to tack him up!"

"That's a good idea," Granny said, squeezing Jessa's shoulder. "Let's sit over here on this box thing." She pointed at a section of a wall jump.

"That's a jump, Granny."

"Surely you don't mean you jump over this? It's very solid!" she added, kicking the wooden section with her toe. "This riding is so dangerous. I don't know how you do it! Horses are so big!"

There was no point in trying to explain to Granny about riding. Jessa had tried before. Granny fell into the category of people who were not, in any way, horsey. She thought horses were big, scary, and smelly.

"When I was a little girl, a cart-horse bit me in the arm. Did I ever tell you that story?"

"Yes. Rebel doesn't bite. He's very sweet."

"No such thing as a sweet horse, I'd say. What are they doing now?"

"Rising trot. Molly's on the wrong diagonal," Jessa added, somewhat smugly.

"The wrong what?"

"Diagonal. See how Rebel's outside foreleg is coming forward—now . . . now . . . now . . ."

"I don't know what you're looking at! I thought horses had left and right legs like anyone else."

"The outside leg is the one beside the fence. The

outside of the ring."

"I see. So, what's his biagonal?"

"Diagonal. See how Molly is rising up and down? That's called posting. Molly is supposed to go up when Rebel's outside foreleg comes forward."

Mrs. Bailey shouted instructions in her loud, do-as-you're-told, teaching voice. "Change the rein coming across the diagonal."

"Mrs. Bailey is talking about the diagonal, too?" Granny was trying hard to follow what was happening in the ring.

"Not exactly. That's a different diagonal."

"So, now Molly's doing the other kind of diagonal properly?"

Molly had, in fact, sat twice in the middle of the ring in order to change her posting, but since she had started out on the wrong diagonal, she still wasn't doing it correctly.

"No."

"But look how she's coming up when his right leg comes forward."

"Yes, but now she's going the other way, so she should be rising with the outside leg . . . his left fore."

"Oh for goodness sake. Never mind!"

"Check your diagonal, Molly!" Mrs. Bailey bellowed.

Molly bounced twice and made the correction.

"There," said Jessa. Rebel had settled into a nice, animated working trot.

"Urge him forward a little but don't throw away your contact . . . good! See how he's starting to soften and bend a little?"

"What is she talking about now?" Granny was mystified.

"See how his nose isn't sticking up any more?"

"Yes. I suppose so."

"Well, that's good."

"Now try a few strides of sitting trot . . . there you go.

107

Don't tip forward!"

"Why isn't she bouncing up and down any more?"

"She's not supposed to."

"And back to rising trot and circle at C."

This time, Molly picked up the correct diagonal the first try.

"Excellent!"

Jessa had to admit the little girl looked pretty good on Rebel. She looked to be about half Jessa's size.

"And, prepare for canter . . ."

Jessa's grandmother stiffened beside her on the wall. "Oh my! He's galloping! Will she fall off?"

Though it irritated her to admit it, Molly didn't look like she was about to take a tumble. Her seat was pretty good for a little kid. "She'll be fine. Rebel knows what he's doing."

As Rebel cantered around the ring, Jessa ached with longing. She wanted to be aboard so badly she could hardly stand it! Without realizing it, she picked up an imaginary pair of reins and sat up straight as if she were riding around the ring instead of Molly.

"Okay! That's enough for today—give him a long rein and then Jessa will take him out on the trail to cool him out. Good job, Molly!"

Rebel took full advantage of the loose reins and stretched his neck until his nose nearly brushed the ground as he walked.

"What do you think?" Mrs. Bailey asked. "They get along very well together, don't they?"

Jessa didn't answer. She swung her feet and thunked her heels against the hollow wooden wall.

"You know, I was thinking . . . there is another horse here at the barn who could use some work."

Jessa looked up at Mrs. Bailey, who was watching Molly thoughtfully. What other horse did Mrs. Bailey mean? Billy Jack the old mule? That couldn't be right.

Cheryl was helping to exercise him. Sienna was still very green and didn't jump. Neither did Brandy, the pinto. Besides, Betty King, his owner, was training for some long-distance ride so he wasn't exactly available.

Marjorie Hamilton's gorgeous Morgan mare could do just about anything. That was largely because Marjorie rode her six days a week and during the summer went to horse shows just about every weekend.

So, who was left?

"Ever since I hurt my backside, I haven't been able to ride Jasmine, except on very gentle trail rides."

"Jasmine?" Jessa gasped. She hadn't even considered Jasmine, Mrs. Bailey's pride and joy. "Jasmine?"

"That is her name, yes. What's wrong, you don't want to ride her?" Mrs. Bailey sounded hurt.

"Yes! It's just . . . I . . ." Jessa couldn't speak. Jasmine was an amazing chestnut mare, a big, beautiful warmblood with lots of scope and tremendous power.

"You would let me try Jasmine?"

"Under supervision, of course. I tell you, it's not doing her any good standing around in her paddock all day. I've been lunging her, but it would do her a world of good to be ridden. What do you say?"

A nod was all Jessa could manage. "Well, here's your pony. Off you go on a trail ride."

Jessa glared at Molly. "Thank you," she said curtly and snatched the reins from the other girl. She bit her tongue rather than say anything else to Molly.

"He's a great pony," Molly offered.

"I know. I've been riding him a lot longer than you have."

Jessa put on her riding helmet and hopped up on Rebel.

"Jessa—wait!" Her grandmother looked worried. "Should you be going out on the trail by yourself?"

"Never a great idea," agreed Mrs. Bailey.

"But—"

"No buts, Jessa." Her grandmother sounded uncharacteristically stern. "What if you go low? Do you have a juice with you?"

Jessa shook her head. She hadn't thought about that. Her pockets weren't big enough to hold a container of juice.

"What about glucose tablets? Do you have any of those with you?"

Guiltily, Jessa shook her head. She had meant to bring the tablets, but in the rush to get to the barn had forgotten them on her bedside table.

"I have juice and cookies in my handbag," Granny said, patting the big sack she lugged around with her everywhere. "Your mother wouldn't let me out of the house without supplies!"

Jessa looked at her grandmother askance. *Surely she wasn't suggesting that Jessa ride with that handbag around her neck? Maybe she could tie it to the saddle somehow. . . .*

As if reading her mind, Granny said, "I feel like a walk myself. Why don't I just stroll along with you—just in case you need anything?"

Jessa opened her mouth to speak and then thought better of it. *Going on a trail ride with her grandmother to take care of her? That was a bit much. On the other hand, carrying that handbag would be more than a little awkward and with her luck, she'd run into someone like Rachel or Jeremy on the trail and then she'd never hear the end of it.*

"I have an idea!" Mrs. Bailey said. "Why don't you ride my old bicycle? It's not in wonderful shape, but if you stick to the Dark Creek Railway trail, the going is pretty flat. That way Jessa won't have to ride so slowly. You can pop your bag into the basket."

A few minutes later Jessa's grandmother wobbled off down the long driveway. Jessa stifled a giggle and squeezed Rebel's sides. He stepped forward eagerly, happy to be heading off on a trail ride. His step on the gravel of the driveway was light and sure. "Oh Rebel, I sure missed you," Jessa crooned as she reached forward and patted his neck.

He took advantage of her momentary distraction and stretched sideways to snatch a mouthful of grass.

"You goof! You haven't changed a bit! Always thinking with your tummy!"

She clucked to him and he picked up a trot. The bicycle had been a brilliant idea. If Granny had been on foot, Jessa and Rebel wouldn't have been able to go faster than a very slow walk. They made their way along Dark Creek Road and then cut across to the Railway Trail.

It felt great to be trotting along the familiar trail once again. Trees and bushes on either side slid back past Rebel. Above her, the taller trees formed a canopy so it seemed like they were riding through a cool, leafy tunnel.

Granny pedalled along easily, glancing back every now and then over her shoulder to see how they were doing.

Jasmine. What a thought! In her daydreams, Jessa had fantasized that someday she would be allowed to ride the chestnut mare. Even as she trotted along, she imagined she was astride the much larger horse and wondered how it would feel.

Her vision clouded a little when she thought of all the things that could go wrong. Jasmine was much bigger, younger, and more powerful than Rebel. She was used to being ridden by one person and one person only— Mrs. Bailey. *What if Jasmine didn't like Jessa? What if Jessa couldn't ride her? What if Jasmine bolted and took off with her? Then what? Would she be able to kick Molly off Rebel and make things go back to the way they had been before?*

"Granny?"

The feeling of hunger overcame Jessa without warning. She pulled Rebel to a stop. Her heart pounded and she felt shaky.

"The juice?"

Jessa nodded and gulped down the whole juice when

her grandmother handed it to her.

"Here, have a couple of these cookies, too. That's what your mother said."

Jessa didn't argue. She crunched her way through the cookies so fast she barely tasted them.

It didn't take long for her to start feeling better. "Thanks, Granny."

Her grandmother nodded and patted her leg. "Are you all right? You looked very pale!"

"I think so. But maybe we should go back."

"Good idea. I only have a couple of cookies left in my bag. And no more juice."

Jessa turned her pony around. Somehow she had thought she would have more warning before she went low. Before she had an insulin reaction. The terms were becoming familiar to her, but having to worry constantly about carrying enough food and drink with her still seemed very strange.

She was very, very glad her grandmother had brought along juice and cookies. *What would have happened if Jessa had been alone on the trail? What if she had gone low so quickly she didn't have time to stop and eat and drink?* The nurse had told her that sometimes when people went low they got so confused they couldn't figure out how to pour a glass of juice.

Jessa bit her bottom lip and encouraged Rebel to walk quickly towards home. Granny didn't have much food left. Jessa sure didn't want to be caught out on the trail without enough supplies to revive her if she went low again.

Tears stung at her eyes. *Obviously, she would never be able to ride the way she used to. Her days of freedom were over.*

Chapter Fifteen

"That didn't take long!" Mrs. Bailey held Rebel while Jessa ran up her stirrups. "You just missed Molly—her mother picked her up. That's too bad! You could have apologized for your rude behaviour earlier."

Jessa didn't respond to Mrs. Bailey's accusation. She led Rebel to the cross-ties and slipped the bridle off.

Mrs. Bailey's sharp blue eyes followed her every motion as she took off Rebel's saddle and started grooming him. "Jessa—it's not Molly's fault you're outgrowing Rebel. It happens to everyone sooner or later. I'm sure if you rode Jasmine you'd see what a great horse she is. Would you like to try her?"

"Right now?"

"Sure."

"Well, I'd like to, but . . ."

"I'm afraid we don't have any more juice with us, and Jessa needs to have dinner in . . ." Granny checked her watch. "She needs to eat in about an hour. That doesn't really give us much time."

"Food? I have lots of food up at the house. Juice, even."

"It's not just the food. I can't eat dinner without insulin. And we didn't bring my blood-testing kit, or needles, or insulin or anything."

"Oh, of course. I'm sorry! How daft of me."

"It's okay. I can ride her another day."

"I hope you're not too disappointed."

Jessa shook her head and loosened the girth. She wasn't disappointed, actually. In fact, she was sort of relieved. Jasmine was a very intimidating horse. She was huge, for one thing: 16.3 hands. That was a lot bigger than Rebel who was supposed to be 14 hands, but who Jessa suspected was a little less than that.

Besides all that, Mrs. Bailey treated her horse like royalty. Jessa knew the older woman was a total perfectionist in everything she did with Jasmine. It would probably take Jessa six hours just to clean the tack properly after each ride.

"What time would be good for you tomorrow?" Mrs. Bailey asked.

"How about right after lunch, Jessa?" Granny suggested. "We could pack some extra food so you don't have to cut your ride short or worry about anything."

Jessa nodded at her grandmother. She couldn't think of a reasonable excuse *not* to come to the barn. "Okay. I guess we could come down after lunch. How about one o'clock?"

"Sounds good to me. Walter will be here, too. He's looking forward to seeing you again, Jessa."

"Jessa? Telephone! It's Cheryl."

"Coming! Okay, Romeo—get up!"

Jessa ran up the back steps into the kitchen when her mother called. Her dog stayed where he was, lying in the shade under the apple tree.

"Hello?"

"Hi, it's me. What are you doing?"

"Training Romeo. He's still staying, even though I told him he could get up."

On the other end of the phone, Cheryl laughed.

"Your dog is nuts!"

"That's why you phoned? To call my dog names?"

"No. To find out how your ride went today and to talk about our birthday party."

"My ride was very short because that Molly was having a lesson. Where were you, anyway? I thought you were going to come to the barn."

"My daahling mother decided, in all her wisdom, that I needed a haircut more than I needed to ride."

Despite the mock dramatic tone, Jessa could tell that her friend wasn't impressed about having someone else change her riding plans. It was an irritation Jessa understood well.

"Do you have a date figured out for the party?"

"July 26." Cheryl switched back to her matter-of-fact planning voice. "We can have a sleepover party. Mom said we could put up tents out in the backyard. Oh, and she said to ask you what you can eat. Unless you want to organize the food."

"What I can eat?" Jessa felt a little left behind. Cheryl seemed to have been doing a lot of planning without her.

"In honour of your diabetes, we're not having cake. But we have to figure something out that doesn't taste disgusting. I haven't had a chance yet to get cookbooks out of the library."

"I can eat lots of stuff."

"But not birthday cake, right?"

"Well, not sugary cake with gobs of icing, no. But maybe there are other kinds of cake I can have."

In the doorway of the kitchen, Jessa's mother pushed her eyebrows together and then disappeared into the living room. She reappeared a minute later waving a diabetic cookbook at Jessa.

"Hang on a second—my mom is looking for a recipe."

"You have a cookbook with desserts in it?"

"Of course. You don't think diabetics go through life without ever eating dessert, do you?"

"Of course not. I know that. Can you bring the book to my place? We could have a party with all diabetic foods in it—if you think other people will eat that stuff."

"That stuff? It's just regular food, more or less. Sure. I'll bring the book. And Romeo, if that's okay." The dog was still snoozing in the grass.

"Fine. See you in five."

"Cinnamon-Apple Cupcakes?"

Jessa wrinkled up her nose. "Boring. That's not birthday food."

"Strawberry Cream Fancies?"

"Gross. Look, it has cream cheese in it."

"Here—this sounds perfect. Angel Mud Cake. How do you feel, by the way?"

Jessa ignored the question and looked at the picture of a fancy layer cake.

"Let me see." Jessa skimmed through the recipe. "Mmmmm . . . that sounds good." The recipe involved angel food cake and a thick layer of diet chocolate pudding.

"Here's what we'll do. On the day of the party, you come over early and we can make the cake before everyone else gets here," Cheryl said.

"Fine." There was no point in arguing when Cheryl was in organizing mode. "Who else is coming?"

Cheryl pulled out her list. "Midori. Sarah. Bridget. And Alicia from the drama club. That's it so far. Do you want to invite anyone else?"

"We should invite Rachel."

Cheryl's eyes bugged out. "Why?"

"She invited us to her party."

"True—but only because her mother made her invite

all the horsey girls in the class!"

"Yeah, and my mother thinks we should do the same." Jessa hesitated before continuing. "Remember how Rachel got really hurt feelings last year when I didn't invite her to my bowling party?"

Cheryl shrugged, unconvinced. "She's such a jerk."

"Sometimes," Jessa nodded. Generally, Rachel Blumen drove her nuts. Her family lived on a large horse farm where they bred Arabian show horses. Rachel's own horse, Gazelle, was a gorgeous grey mare who looked like one of those flashy Arabians featured in calendars. Rachel never missed an opportunity to brag about her perfect horse or to put down Jessa's "pony." Now, incredibly, Jessa found herself defending her snooty classmate.

"Just because people don't like her doesn't mean we have to be mean to her."

"People are mean to her because she's mean to them," Cheryl countered.

Jessa began to feel self-righteous. "If she had some 'real' friends, maybe she would be nicer."

"You're not suggesting we should be her real friends?"

Jessa didn't know quite what she was suggesting any more.

"Well, we should at least invite her to the party."

"Fine. Then we'll have to invite Monika, too."

"Fine. I don't mind Monika." Monika Jacobowski was slightly crazy. Her motto was "Faster! Faster!" She was always tearing around on her Anglo-Arab, Silver Dancer. She loved jumping, but it seemed to Jessa it was only a matter of time before she had a serious crash.

Jessa watched Cheryl add the two names to the list. She sure didn't feel like she had won the argument. Mostly, she regretted opening her mouth in the first place.

She surveyed the finished list, and wondered how

everyone would get along. First, there were the riding girls—Rachel, Monika, and Sarah. Sarah Blackwater was the most serious rider. She had her eye on the Olympic Equestrian Team. She loved dressage and spent hours and hours training with Anansi, one of the top dressage horses at the Arbutus Lane Equestrian Centre.

Then there was Midori, who was from Japan and loved gymnastics. When Midori had first come to Kenwood Elementary, both Jessa and Cheryl had helped her settle in.

Bridget Anderson had occasional riding lessons, but preferred rock climbing and sea kayaking to riding. Unfortunately, there weren't a lot of other kids who shared her interests. The only other kid at school Jessa could think of who ever went kayaking was Blake Ryerson. Jessa could see why Bridget wouldn't want to spend a lot of time with him since he was so shy he hardly ever said more than a word or two, and then only when a teacher asked him directly.

And finally, there was Alicia, the only person Jessa didn't know very well. Alicia didn't ride and had been in the other Grade Six homeroom.

"Are you listening to me, Matey?"

"What? Sorry, what did you say?"

Cheryl had changed to a throaty, tough-sounding brogue.

"There's hidden treasure about, don't you know."

"What are you talking about?"

"Gold, me lassie." She switched to her normal voice. "We can have a hidden treasure party and all come dressed up as pirates."

Jessa groaned. "Can't you ever do anything without getting dressed up?"

Just because Cheryl was theatrically inclined didn't mean she had to force everyone else to act silly.

"It will be fun! We can go to Widow's Watch

Provincial Park and have a barbecue—you can eat barbecued food, right?"

"Sure. Hotdogs, hamburgers, whatever."

Cheryl hardly listened, she was so caught up in her ideas. "We can hide some clues in the park and then whoever finds the treasure first wins!"

"When are we going to hide clues?" Jessa felt as though she were several steps behind.

"Well, we can't do that part because otherwise we can't hunt for the treasure."

"So who's going to do the clues?"

"I have it all figured out. Anthony and Bernie can do it for us. They'll come up with some great clues."

Anthony was Cheryl's older brother and Bernie his outrageous girlfriend. She wanted to be a sculptor and live in New York City. Jessa could only imagine what kind of complicated clues those two would come up with!

"If they do the clues," Cheryl rattled on, "we can make the cake and the food. That way we can be in the hunt, too."

"We can't win the prize, though. Since we're the hostesses."

"I've never understood why the hostess can't win the prize!" Cheryl poked out her bottom lip. "You're right though. We could split into teams. So, I'll have to get some small prizes so each member of the winning team gets something."

Cheryl dug around in her desk and found a piece of not-too-crumpled paper. She sketched a map of Widow's Watch Park.

"We could have the barbecue here . . . and then the treasure hunt could be in this area, over here." She drew an X on the page. "X marks the spot. Oh! We need to design invitations! Can you draw a skull and cross bones?"

Cheryl jumped into action and pulled paper, coloured pens, crayons, ribbons, scraps of fabric, and feathers from an overflowing cardboard box in her closet. The girls set to work and before long they couldn't see the floor of Cheryl's room.

They were deeply engrossed in making party invitations when the bedroom door swung open and Anthony appeared with a tray of cheese and crackers.

"Hi, Jessa. How do you feel?"

Jessa eyed the tray warily when Cheryl's brother pushed aside a heap of buttons and seashells.

"I hope this is okay for food. According to this pamphlet . . ."

Anthony pulled a piece of folded paper from his back pocket. Jessa recognized it immediately. *Diabetes 1-2-3: A Quick Guide for Teachers, Friends and Caretakers.*

"Where did you get that?" The last time Jessa had seen the pamphlet was at the hospital in Calgary. There had been a stack of them on Nurse Alice's desk.

"Your mom brought it over."

"We've all read it," Cheryl added proudly. "So, don't eat any of this unless it's time for your snack," she added bossily.

"My mother gave this to you?" Jessa's mouth sagged open. *Now she came with an instruction manual!*

"It's 7:30," Anthony said.

Jessa pushed the tray aside. "Well, thanks, Anthony, but I don't have to eat again until bedtime."

Anthony ran his hand through his spiky red hair. He looked a little disappointed.

"I'll leave it here . . . just in case." The door closed quietly behind him and neither girl said anything until they heard him close the door to his own room down the hall.

"People should frame these!" Cheryl said brightly, holding up Rachel's invitation. "What amazing works of art!" Jessa's dour look was impossible to miss. Her whole mood had been spoiled and even Cheryl's goofy chatter did little to alleviate her grumpiness.

"Are you sure you feel comfortable about sleeping over at Cheryl's house?"

Jessa picked at her salad. From the minute Cheryl had first said the word "sleepover," Jessa had been feeling a little nervous. What if she went low during the night? What if her blood sugar was high and she had to keep getting up to go to the bathroom?

"It will probably be okay. We'll be pretty close to her house."

"You could keep some juice and glucose tablets near your pillow," Granny suggested.

"What about my shot, though?"

"You could phone me in the evening, if you had a question about the dose. . . ."

Though they were all trying to be calm about it, nobody at the dining room table sounded overly enthusiastic about the whole idea of Jessa staying overnight.

"I'm sure it will be fine," Jessa said, trying to convince herself as much as anyone else.

"I'll get it," her mother said when the phone rang. "Oh, hi, Cheryl. We were just talking about the party. Yes, she's here."

"Hi, birthday girl," Jessa said, taking the phone.

"Hi, late birthday girl," Cheryl answered. "Guess what!! I just had the most brilliant idea! There's a campground at Widow's Watch, right?"

"Yeah. Over near the beach."

"So, I was thinking we should camp out at the park! Then we wouldn't have to leave after the barbecue and it would be more like an adventure!"

"Camp out at the park?"

"Everything's arranged! Bernie and Anthony agreed to come with us, so we'll be supervised, but no parents!! Doesn't that sound like an excellent party? We can stay up late and have a bonfire and tell ghost stories. Anthony is *really* good at telling scary stories!"

"Yeah. It sounds like fun. For you guys."

"What do you mean?"

"I guess I won't be coming. You can just have your party by yourself and I'll do something different for mine—maybe in a couple of weeks."

"What!?"

Jessa hung up the phone and sat down again at the table, fighting back tears. "Cheryl's going to have a camp-out at the park."

"Oh dear," her mother said.

"I guess I'm not going to the party," Jessa said glumly. It had been scary enough to think about sleeping over in Cheryl's backyard, never mind in tents in a campground. Cheryl might be glad that the party would be free of parents, but Jessa wasn't. Now she was back to square one with her own birthday plans.

"Oh, Jessa." Jessa felt her mother's arms around her shoulders. "I'm so sorry."

"You don't have to miss the whole party, do you?" Granny said. "You could go for the treasure hunt and barbecue and then come home. . . ."

Jessa bit her lip. *It wasn't fair! Why should she have to miss out on all the fun of giggling in the tents until dawn?*

"As a matter of fact, you could stay until quite late so you didn't miss out on the ghost stories or anything. I could pick you up at eleven o'clock. As long as you promise not to sleep in the next morning!" her mother added.

"You could even go back to the park in the morning and join the rest of the girls for camp breakfast! I could drive you back if your mom is working."

"You'd probably be the only one who gets any sleep!" Jessa's mother added.

"True. They should probably call those parties wake-overs," Jessa said, feeling a little less discouraged.

"You'd better call Cheryl back," her mom said, but right then the phone rang again.

"Hi, Jessa?"

"Hi. I was just going to call."

"Don't worry about anything! We can change the plans. We'll just have a regular party here at the house. Or maybe go bowling. No sleepover—nothing. You decide what you'd like to do and I'll agree—but you *have* to come!"

"Hold on! You don't have to change any plans. I can come to just about everything. I just won't sleep at the campground, that's all." Jessa explained everything and at the other end of the line, Cheryl heaved a huge sigh of relief.

"Great! If you don't mind not sleeping out there, we could still do just about everything together. You barely have to miss a thing!"

"I *do* mind," Jessa said. "But it beats not going at all."

"Oh, I have to tell you something." Cheryl sounded anxious and Jessa wondered what bomb her friend was going to drop next.

"What?" she asked cautiously.

"It's about the treasure hunt. You'll have to be Rachel's partner."

"What! Why?"

"Well, you and I can't be together because we're both hostesses so we have to share ourselves around. And Monika doesn't get along with Alicia—well, more like Alicia doesn't like Monika that much. . . ."

Jessa groaned. Choosing partners was always so complicated, but even so, she didn't expect Cheryl's next piece of logic.

"And I found out that Rachel has been at Wilderness Camp so she knows how to cope with . . . um . . . she knows what to do in case of a medical emergency."

Jessa opened her mouth to protest that she wasn't planning on having a medical emergency, but Cheryl kept on talking.

"Hey, I don't want to hear any complaints about getting stuck with Rachel! You're the one who insisted on inviting her!"

Cheryl had a point. Jessa tried desperately to think of some other reason why she couldn't be Rachel's partner, but Cheryl clearly did not intend to discuss the matter further.

"I nearly forgot—I meant to ask you whether you could go on a trail ride tomorrow."

"Well, I guess so. That sounds like fun." Jessa was just as happy to think about riding instead of Rachel. "Oh, wait a second. I'm not riding Rebel. I don't think Mrs. Bailey will let Jasmine out of her sight."

"Oh, right. Is Molly riding?"

Jessa groaned. "Probably."

Cheryl didn't say anything, but Jessa had a nasty feeling that her friend was thinking about calling Molly to see if she could go on the trail ride.

"Well, maybe I'll see you at the barn!" Cheryl chirped.

"Yeah. Maybe."

Chapter Sixteen

"Blood test?"

"Yes."

"Snack?"

"Yes."

"Feeling okay?"

"Yes."

Jessa's mother leaned over, kissed Jessa on the forehead, and tucked the light quilt up under her chin.

Somehow, her mother had fallen out of the habit of tucking her in every night. Jessa hadn't even realized it until they had come home from the hospital and her mother had started up the routine again. Now, though, she ran through a quick diabetic checklist every night to make sure Jessa had eaten her snack, tested her blood, and felt okay.

"I'm glad Granny's here," Jessa said. Her mother pushed a stray strand of hair off Jessa's cheek.

"Me, too. We haven't seen nearly enough of your grandmother since the divorce."

"Maybe she can come visit more often now," Jessa said.

"That would be nice, wouldn't it? Isn't it silly that you had to get sick before we could get organized for a proper long visit? We've talked about Granny coming over for ages, but somehow, the time just slipped away. Well, she's here now and that's what matters."

Jessa's mother smoothed the blanket gently and said, "Good night, sweetie."

The door closed and Jessa listened in the dark as her mother's footsteps retreated down the narrow stairs leading from her attic bedroom. Her thoughts drifted, shifting from Cheryl's party, to an image of having her shot before dinner, to Jasmine.

Jasmine. Jessa imagined herself sitting astride the powerful horse, urging her into an extended trot, smoothly collecting her and then feeling the thrust of the mare's haunches as she propelled herself into a canter. Jasmine could do flying changes and counter canter, leg yields, haunches in, and turns on the forehand. Not only was she competing in the medium levels in dressage, she was also a wonderful jumper, easily clearing 4' 6". Mrs. Bailey said her sire was a top cross-country performer and that Jasmine had inherited his boldness.

In her mind's eye, Jessa urged Jasmine into a gallop and flew across an open field. Together they plunged off a bank, picked up speed, and leaped over a big log into the water. They galloped through the water and then up a bank on the far side before tackling a large brush jump angling across the side of a hill.

With a start, Jessa realized she hadn't once thought about Rebel. "Sorry, Rebel," she whispered under her breath. *How could she have betrayed her beloved pony like that?* Jessa vowed to bring her pony a special treat of carrots, to prove to him that he was still number one in her books.

Though she tried to quiet her thoughts and fall asleep, images of Jasmine, brilliant rides, big fences, and fancy ribbons and trophies kept pushing themselves into her mind and it was a long time before she slept.

"Hi there, Jessa! The princess is waiting for you!"

When Jessa arrived at the barn, Jasmine was standing in the cross-ties. "Hello, baaaaby," Mrs. Bailey crooned. "Jessa's going to ride you today, so you be a goooood girl, okay, darling?"

It never ceased to amaze Jessa how Mrs. Bailey seemed to undergo a complete personality transplant whenever she was around Jasmine. Usually, Mrs. Bailey was a little on the gruff side, strict about barn rules and rather bossy. But when she talked to her horse, she turned totally silly.

"Here you go, lovey. Look what Mumsy-wumsy has for you."

Jasmine eagerly lipped the tiny Fisherman's Friend cough candy from Mrs. Bailey's open palm. Jasmine bobbed her head up and down in appreciation and smacked her lips as she worked on the potent morsel.

"I tell you, that horse of yours has terrible breath!" Walter Walters emerged from the tack room, cleaning Jasmine's bridle. "Howdy, Jessa! Good to see you again! I hear you are going to try Lady Jasmine?"

Jessa nodded and took the stiff brush Mrs. Bailey offered her.

"Oooooh, Jasmine, you are a dirty, dirty girl," Mrs. Bailey crooned.

She wasn't kidding. Clouds of dust rose from Jasmine's back as Jessa and Mrs. Bailey set to work grooming.

"She's so big!" It was a silly thing to say, but the mare seemed like she was twice the size of Rebel.

"Where is Rebel?" Jessa asked.

"Cheryl and Molly left a little while ago. They went out on a trail ride."

Jessa peered over at Billy Jack's paddock in disbelief. Sure enough, it was empty. A twinge of jealously squeezed in her chest. *So, Cheryl had been planning to arrange a trail ride after all. Some friend!* Jessa hoped they would be gone for a long time so she wouldn't have to speak to Cheryl. She didn't trust herself to be able to say anything pleasant.

"Be careful there. . . ." Jasmine swished her tail and Mrs. Bailey pointed to a spot on her flank. "She's got a ticklish spot. You have to be very gentle when you brush her there."

Jessa skirted around the trouble spot, leaving it for Mrs. Bailey.

"She's very good about her feet, aren't you, baby?"

Jasmine bobbed her head up and down and Mrs. Bailey gave her a loving pat on the neck. "Oh, you are such a clever girl, aren't you, sweetums?"

The big horse nodded her head again, looking for all the world like she really understood exactly what her owner was saying.

"Shall I bring her saddle out, BB?" Walter offered.

"Thanks, dear. Now, Jessa, leave her tail alone. I'm trying to let it thicken up a bit."

When every last speck of dust had been whisked out of Jasmine's coat, Jessa picked up the saddle and then stood at the horse's side. She looked up helplessly.

"I don't think I can . . ."

"Here. Stand on this," Walter said, bringing a heavy bucket out of the tack room. He turned it upside down with a hollow thunk.

Even up on the bucket, it was tricky to manoeuvre the saddle into place. Not only was Jasmine taller, she was also much wider than Rebel. It was quite a stretch to settle the saddle properly.

"That's a little too far back, dear," said Mrs. Bailey. "Lift it up and forward . . . more . . . . there. Now slide it back a tad so the hair lies flat underneath. Make sure the pad underneath is pulled up under the pommel so it doesn't rub against her withers."

Jessa jiggled and smoothed and adjusted the saddle and pad and then hopped off the stool to deal with the girth. It was nearly twice as long as Rebel's. Jasmine stood quietly while she fastened the buckles. Mrs. Bailey distracted the mare with another cough candy while Jessa snugged the girth.

"I'll do the bridle for you today, shall I?"

Jessa didn't argue. The saddle had been tricky enough. She didn't want to think about the trouble she might have reaching up to bridle Jasmine. Mrs. Bailey had no problems whatsoever. In fact, Jasmine stretched her head forward and down, poking her nose through the headstall.

"That's my goooood girl." With the noseband and throatlatch fastened, Mrs. Bailey handed Jessa the reins.

"Here you go, dear. Take her into the ring and let's see how you do."

Jasmine nudged at Jessa's elbow with her nose. In the sunshine the horse gleamed like a polished penny. "Don't buck me off, okay? And I'll try not to catch you in the mouth or do anything else stupid," Jessa said under her breath, making a deal with Jasmine.

In the ring, Jessa lined Jasmine up with the mounting block. She didn't usually bother to use it when she hopped up on Rebel, but the way Jasmine towered over her, it wasn't just convenient—it was necessary.

Jessa settled gently into the saddle and slipped her feet into the stirrups.

"They'll have to come up a hole or two." Mrs. Bailey adjusted the length on one side while Walter did the other. Jessa felt like a little kid having her first ever riding lesson. She half expected Mrs. Bailey to slip a lead-line on Jasmine!

"That looks better! Right, pick up your reins and off you go."

Jessa gave a little squeeze. Jasmine craned her neck

around and looked up at her as if to say, "That was supposed to be a leg aid? Are you kidding?"

"You'll have to be firm with her. She's not quite as forward as Rebel. You'll have to work a little harder."

Mrs. Bailey wasn't kidding. Keeping the mare at a reasonable forward walk was far more difficult than Jessa had expected. "Rising trot, Jessa!"

Jasmine stumbled forward into a trot, her long stride carrying them around the ring far more quickly than Jessa was used to.

"Jessa! You two are sprawling all over the place! Let's see her working from behind . . . but still at the trot!"

Jessa clenched her teeth. Her attempt to half-halt so she could balance the mare made Jasmine stall right down into the walk.

"Pick up the trot again—you want to create momentum and enthusiasm but not let her run! She's very sensitive in the downward transitions—you can be subtle!"

Jessa tried again. "Jessa! Your position! Where are your legs?"

Jessa concentrated on keeping her heels down and legs on Jasmine's sides. "Keep your hands down! Good heavens, Jessa—what are you doing up there?"

"Steady, Jasmine," Jessa murmured. The big mare's long, swinging stride made her feel unbalanced and awkward. Jasmine leaned into the bit.

"You have to use your legs—push her together from behind. Relax your upper body!"

Was Mrs. Bailey kidding? Relax? Jessa felt like she was in a tug-of-war. *Rebel never pulled like this!*

"Try a few steps of sitting trot."

Jessa sat into the saddle and Jasmine's head flipped up and her back hollowed.

"Back to rising!"

Jessa didn't need to be told. Sitting the sprawling trot

was more than uncomfortable and made her feel like a sack of potatoes bouncing around in the saddle. *How on earth did Mrs. Bailey do it?* When she rode her horse, Jasmine was supple and graceful, a prize-winning example of a highly trained dressage horse.

"Watch your corners! Don't let her fall in like that! More inside leg—support with the outside rein! Walk! Walk! Bring her back to a walk! Use your seat . . . don't pull on her like that. She'll just lean on you!"

Back at the walk, Jessa felt like her legs were going to fall off. What on earth was she doing wrong? Everything, it seemed.

"Rebel sure makes you look good!" Mrs. Bailey remarked. Then she added, kindly, "It's hard to get used to another horse. I think it will be good for you to ride Jasmine for a bit. She won't do a thing properly unless you ask correctly!"

That was certainly true. So far, Jessa couldn't seem to maintain a decent walk, never mind a brilliant trot. *So much for her visions of flying changes and canter pirouettes!*

"Okay, let's start from scratch. Show me a nice square halt and we'll adjust your position."

Now Jessa really did feel like she was back in riding kindergarten.

"Of course she feels very different than Rebel. But the mark of a good rider is to be able to get on any horse, make adjustments, and still ride well."

Mrs. Bailey took hold of Jessa's boot and moved her lower leg back. "Just at the girth, here . . . glance down—can you see your toe? No, don't tip forward— look straight down. Now, do you see your toe?"

"Barely."

"Good. Now, ask her to move forward. Sink deeper into the saddle—don't throw away your hands but yes, let her come forward . . . ask again with your legs . . . good . . . that's a better walk now."

"Shorten your reins a little. Let your hands follow the movement of her head and neck . . . good . . . you don't want to restrict her forward motion. Now, ask her to bend a little, from behind—don't pull on her mouth! Good, better . . ."

For the next half-hour, Jessa concentrated as hard as she could, trying to do exactly as Mrs. Bailey said. By the end of the lesson, Jasmine was managing a respectable working trot. She was far from the top of her form, but at least was no longer zooming around the ring like a completely green, unbalanced horse who had never heard of collection, extension, or even straight halts!

When Jessa finally dismounted, her legs quivered. Only forty-five minutes? Her watch must have stopped!

"Are you okay?" Walter asked when she staggered backwards a couple of steps.

"Oh, my legs," Jessa groaned.

"Just wait until tomorrow," Mrs. Bailey said knowingly.

"I'll give you a hand putting her away. That wasn't too bad, all things considered. When would you like your next lesson?"

"You mean, you'd let me ride her again?"

"Certainly—if you feel up to the challenge."

"I guess so." Jessa didn't feel up to any such challenge. She felt like giving up riding right then and there. She didn't feel great about riding Jasmine at all—instead, she felt completely humiliated, as if she had never had a riding lesson in her entire life. They walked back to the barn and untacked Jasmine.

"She's not a particularly easy horse to ride," Mrs. Bailey admitted. "Not like Rebel. He's a push-button pony, but you are ready to move on. I'm quite sure of that now."

Jessa rubbed the stiff brush over the damp strip where

the girth had been. She didn't say anything, but she didn't agree with Mrs. Bailey. *She wasn't ready to move on. She just wanted her pony back.* Unfortunately, it seemed that today Jessa wasn't even going to be able to see him. Even though she took her time grooming Jasmine and then carefully cleaned her tack before she put it away, there was still no sign of Cheryl and Molly when her mother's car pulled up.

She gave a little wave in reply to Mrs. Bailey when she tipped her hat goodbye, but then sank deep into the passenger seat.

"So, how did it go?"

"Don't ask. Terrible."

"But I thought Jasmine was such a great horse. . . ."

"Yeah, maybe for someone who knows how to ride. I don't want to talk about it. I'm hungry."

A look of concern passed over her mother's face. "Do you need a juice?"

"I don't think so. I just feel hungry."

"You'd better do a blood test."

"Right here?"

"Well, yes. You may not last until you get home. I have to stop for gas on the way."

Reluctantly, Jessa pulled out her testing supplies and did a quick blood test in the car as they drove to the gas station.

"3.6," she reported.

"Have a little bit of juice. That should make you feel a bit better until we can get home for supper." Her mother turned her attention to the gas station attendant. "Could you hurry, please? My daughter is a diabetic and we have to get home to eat!"

"Mom! You didn't have to say that!"

"Well, yes I did. He was being so slow! People don't understand that you have to eat on time!"

Jessa sipped on her juice. There was no point in

pursuing her complaint. Her mother didn't seem to understand how embarrassing it was to have the whole world know about her condition.

"So, what are we having for dinner?"

"Granny has been busy this afternoon. She found a few good recipes in the new cookbook and then went shopping while I was at work. She made some sort of pasta dish. It should be just about ready when we get home."

"Mmmmm . . . I like spaghetti," Jessa agreed. The juice was beginning to work. She felt a little less hungry but still looked forward to having a good meal of her grandmother's cooking. It was a lot more pleasant to think about eating than it was to think about riding.

Chapter Seventeen

"I bet that's Cheryl," Jessa said when the phone rang after dinner.

"Well, are you going to answer it?" her mother asked.

"No. Tell her I don't want to talk to her."

The phone rang again.

"I will tell her no such thing. Are you two fighting again?"

Jessa scowled and didn't answer.

"Answer the phone, Jessa! You are being very rude."

Jessa didn't get up from the table.

The phone rang again and her mother reached for it with a frown in Jessa's general direction. "Hello?"

"Oh, hello, Cheryl. Yes, she's sitting right here. Would you like to talk to her?"

Susan Richardson paid no attention to her daughter's hideous expressions and shaking head. She thrust the phone at Jessa.

"Yes?"

"Hi! How was your lesson? There wasn't anybody around when we got back."

"Awful. I never want to ride that stupid horse again."

At the other end of the line Jessa heard the loud smack of Cheryl popping a bubble gum bubble. "Stupid horse? I thought you were going to ride Jasmine?"

"I did ride Jasmine. I have to go."

"Why? I wanted to talk about our party. Can you

come over?"

"No."

"What's wrong?"

"Why do you want to talk to me about the party? Why don't you talk to Molly? Why don't you have a joint party with *her*?"

"Why would I want to do that? She's just a little kid!"

"I figured you'd want to invite her to go camping, since I can't stay."

"Jessa, I don't know what you're talking about. We went for a trail ride. She's not allowed to go out on the trails alone and we knew you were having a lesson, so we figured we'd get out of your way. Besides, I know how you feel about her and my reading tells me that emotional upsets can cause a diabetic's blood sugars to go haywire."

Jessa resisted the urge to slam the phone down. Luckily, Cheryl changed the subject back to riding.

"So, what happened? Did you fall off?"

"No, I didn't fall off." It was about the only thing that hadn't gone wrong. "Jasmine is just harder to ride than I thought."

"I can relate," said Cheryl. "You know how hard it was for me to figure out how to make old Billy Jack canter on the correct lead."

Jessa had to laugh. Cheryl was a lot better than when she had started riding, but her canter leads were still hit and miss.

"So, how was Rebel?" Jessa blurted out. Just asking the question reminded her of the sad ache she felt inside. It was stronger than ever now that she had tried Jasmine.

"Typical Rebel. He kept trying to eat the grass at the side of the trail. But other than that, he was good. Molly really likes him."

"I'm sure she does. You know, in the olden days horse

thieves were shot."

"Jessa!" Jessa turned away from her mother, who looked appalled at her daughter's uncharitable comment. She lowered her voice and went on.

"I'm not ready for a new horse," she said. "I have to get him back. You have to help me."

"Help you? Help you how?"

"We have to make Molly want to change horses."

"Good luck. Rebel is perfect for her. And you're getting too big to ride him anyway. You said yourself he's getting too stiff in his knees to jump anything much bigger than a cross-pole."

"Look, you weren't there to see my lesson today. It was *baaaaaad*. Jasmine is not the horse for me. I'll never be able to ride her."

"Jessa, you're crazy! You've always wanted to ride her! She's a brilliant horse. You could win every show around if you keep going with her. I bet you could even beat Rachel."

Rachel and her horse, Gazelle, were always in the ribbons.

"Don't you want to beat those two? You could probably even compete with Jeremy!"

"I don't know about that." Jeremy and Caspian were a pretty extraordinary pair. They'd been together for several years and were formidable in three-day eventing circles.

"So Molly isn't coming to your party?"

"Of course not. And it's *our* party and you are going to be there and I need your help! You have to come over and help me make decorations. Ask your mother."

"Decorations? You're going to decorate the campground?"

"But of course! And everyone has to come dressed up as pirates. Mom and Dad said we could go down to the basement and find stuff in the costume storage room."

"Costumes? You expect me to wear a costume?"

"Certainly, daaaahling. So, can you come over?"

"Right now?"

"Yes, right now. Time's a wasting."

Jessa held the phone to her chest. "Can I go over—" Her mother didn't even give her a chance to finish before she nodded.

"I'll be there in five minutes."

Her mother shook her head and pointed at the kitchen sink.

"Make that fifteen minutes. I have to do the dishes first."

"What! Your mother is making you, a poor, sick diabetic, wash dishes? That doesn't seem fair!"

"Try telling her that!" Jessa winked at her mother and hung up the phone.

"What was that all about?"

"Oh, nothing. The quicker I get started, the quicker I'll be done," she said and turned on the hot water.

"Where did she say she'd be?"

"In the campground—she didn't know the site number."

"There's nobody in the office to ask." Jessa's mother leaned out of the car window and read the sign in the window. "'Back at 2:00 p.m.' Well, it's only 1:30."

"Let's just drive around. I'm sure we'll see everyone."

The car rattled forward, creeping along the narrow campground road. Tall trees towered above them, throwing the ground below into cool shade. "Is that them?"

Jessa looked at a family sitting at a picnic table beside two blue tents. "Nope. Wrong dog." Ginger, Cheryl's dog, was a yellowish terrier cross, not a black lab like the dog barking from beside the picnic cooler.

"That must be it! Look at all the balloons!" Cheryl hadn't been kidding about decorating her campsite. The trees all around the site were festooned with balloons and streamers. She ran out into the road and flagged down Jessa's car. "Midori and Alicia are here already. Where's your costume?"

Jessa grimaced. "In my bag."

"The outhouse is over there—but it's really stinky. You can get changed in my tent."

"See you later tonight, Jessa."

"Bye, Mom."

"You have everything? Insulin? Tester? Strips? Syringes? Glucose?"

"Yes, yes, yes." Jessa followed Cheryl towards the tent. She didn't turn around to wave when she heard the car drive off. *She and her mother had carefully checked that everything was in Jessa's bag before they left the house. Why did she have to behave like such a worrywart?*

"Hi, Jessa!" Midori waved from where she stood balanced on one leg on top of the picnic table. She couldn't resist leaping up on things and practising her leaps, turns, handstands, and splits.

"Agh!" Jessa yelped when she stuck her head into the tent. She had come face to face with Alicia, who was on her way out of the tent and dressed in full pirate costume.

"Nice greeting," Alicia quipped, as the two girls crawled past each other.

"Need a hand in there?" Cheryl offered.

"No, thanks." Jessa struggled to change into the pair of pirate pants she had borrowed from Cheryl's costume collection. The white blouse with puffy sleeves belonged to Jessa's mother, who had reluctantly agreed to let Jessa wear it out in the forest. Granny had sewed an eye patch, and Jessa had found a red bandana in her closet. She wrapped it around her head and then fastened on a single, large, clip-on hoop earring.

When she emerged from the tent she was transformed.

"Wow!" said Cheryl appreciatively. "For someone who hates getting dressed up, you look great."

"Thanks," Jessa mumbled. "What the heck are you doing?"

Cheryl was busy strapping her ankle up to her thigh with a belt. When her leg was folded in half and fastened securely, she slipped into a pair of billowy pants that fastened just below the knee. She then took something that vaguely resembled an oversized bowling pin and buckled it under her knee. When she stood up on her one good leg, it looked just like she had a peg leg.

"That looks great," Alicia said, admiring the effect.

Cheryl donned her pirate hat and picked up a walking stick from the table.

"Arrrrr . . . ye mateys!" she growled with a pirate accent. "Where's Cracker?"

Midori handed Cheryl a stuffed green parrot. Cheryl fastened the bird to her shoulder with a couple of safety pins. The picture was perfect. Cheryl looked like she should be in a movie.

"Can you walk?"

"Aye! Aye! Stand aside!" Cheryl half hopped and half hobbled, leaning heavily on her stick. "Hail yonder ship!"

Rachel's dad's Mercedes pulled up at the campsite, and she and Monika climbed out of the back seat. Both were dressed in full pirate regalia. As they threw their sleeping bags out of the trunk and carried presents to the table, two more cars pulled up. Sarah and Bridget scrambled out of their vehicles and unloaded all their gear.

Bridget was dressed as a pirate, but Sarah wore a long,

flowing gown, and a tiara glittered on her head.

"What kind of pirate are you supposed to be?" Monika asked.

Sarah sighed delicately. "I'm a fair maiden. You pirates are supposed to rescue me."

"Take you captive," leered Captain Cheryl.

When the two cars drove off, everyone gathered around the picnic table and exchanged murmurs of appreciation. Jessa had to admit the costumes looked great.

"So your parents really aren't here?" Rachel asked.

"Parents? Any pirate worth her salt doesn't have parents!"

"Anthony and Bernie are hiding clues in the woods," explained Alicia. "They've been gone for ages."

"Ooooh, me aching stump," groaned Cheryl, sitting on the bench.

"When are you opening the presents?" asked Rachel.

"What about food?" Alicia asked.

Cheryl glanced at Jessa. "The galley is loaded with provisions, mateys. Potato chippies for elevenses, and cake made by matey Jessa and me ear-lie in the morning for tea time at eight bells."

Jessa glanced at her watch. She had no idea what actual time corresponded to eight bells.

"Elevenses is in the morning," Bridget said. "Tea time is in the afternoon."

"Arrrr, who are you questioning?" Cheryl snarled, waving her walking stick under Bridget's nose. "I'll have no insubordination from you lot of scoundrels!"

"And isn't eight bells in the morning?" Bridget went on, ignoring Cheryl's challenge.

"We'll ruddy well eat when our bellies tell us!" Cheryl let out a wicked cackle that sounded more like a witch than a pirate, and all the girls whooped with laughter.

Midori hopped down from the table and fished a big

bag of potato chips out of a box full of food. She ripped open the bag and eight hands reached for chips. Jessa took a handful and then caught Cheryl's good eye, the one not covered with a patch. The concern was unmistakable and Jessa gritted her teeth. She took one chip and put the rest on the table. Soundlessly, Cheryl scooped up Jessa's chips and added them to her own pile.

"Ahoy there, mateys!" Anthony's voice called from somewhere in the forest.

"Ahoy there!" Cheryl bellowed in reply. A moment later, two tall pirates emerged from the trees.

"Captain," the taller, red-haired one growled. "We were scouting out the lay of the land and found these."

Pirate Anthony pulled several rolls of parchment from his pocket.

"What be these? Could they be treasure maps?"

"Aye aye, Cap'n! Treasure maps indeed. Hidden gold, I daresay!"

Cheryl took the four maps. "We'll have better luck finding the treasure if we split up. Midori and Sarah." She read out two names written on the outside of one of the rolls. "You will set off together to find the secret clues."

She picked up the next scroll. "Bridget and Monika. Alicia and Me. And Jessa and Rachel."

Even though Jessa knew about the planned pairs, she still felt a twinge of irritation.

"Each map has six clues. If you follow the directions carefully, you should find treasure at the end of your search." Anthony had dropped his pirate accent to explain what the girls were supposed to do. "You can look anywhere in Widow's Watch Park except in other people's private campsites. That includes the picnic areas, the woods, the playground, and the beach. There's no time limit but we figure it shouldn't take much longer than an hour to find all the clues, get the treasure, and rendezvous at the secret meeting place. Then we'll come back here to our campsite and start getting a fire going for hot dogs later. Any questions?"

Monika spoke up. "What if someone else finds the treasure first? How will we know we found the right spot?"

Bernie grinned. "We've been busy. There are four different maps, four different sets of clues, and four different treasures. There's a bonus prize for the team that finds their treasure first."

Jessa looked appreciatively at the two older pirates. They had sure gone to a lot of trouble. It was times like this that Jessa really wished she had an older brother or sister instead of being an only child.

"Rachel. Come here a minute."

Cheryl hobbled over behind the tents and beckoned to Rachel. Jessa started to follow but Cheryl glared at her and said, "I need to talk to Rachel privately."

Chapter Eighteen

Wounded, Jessa retreated to the picnic table. The others were already poring over their maps. Jessa would have liked to study hers, too, but Rachel had taken it with her to her private conference. *What on earth were they talking about?*

Cheryl and Rachel looked very serious. Every now and then Rachel looked over towards Jessa and then nodded. Cheryl tugged a piece of paper from her pocket and gave it to Rachel. Even at a distance, Jessa recognized the annoying *Diabetes 1-2-3* flyer. She turned her back on them in disgust. If they hadn't been out at the park, she would have got up right then and there and walked home.

"Ready?" Rachel sat beside Jessa at the table and pulled the map from her pocket. She smoothed it out in front of them and leaned forward, tucking a long strand of her dark hair behind her ear.

"What were you talking about?" Jessa pretended she hadn't seen the flyer.

"Nothing," Rachel said just a tad too quickly and innocently for Jessa's liking. "Talking about dinner. Cheryl wants me to help with the cooking because she knows I have lots of experience with wilderness food preparation."

"You do?"

"Sure. I went to an outdoors camp earlier this

summer. In Arizona. We did mountain climbing and wilderness survival and river rafting."

"Oh." Jessa found it hard to picture Miss Perfect hanging off a whitewater raft, screaming her lungs out.

"We also did map reading."

"Which way is north?" Jessa asked. "Where are we on this map?" Since she was obviously stuck with both the treasure hunt and her partner, Jessa figured they might as well try to find the treasure first.

Anthony and Bernie had photocopied official park maps and then drawn over the top of them. They had changed the names of the landmarks. "Widow's Point" was now "Pirate's Point" and "Cedar Beach" was "Buccaneer Sands."

Rachel read out the first clue written in the bottom corner of the treasure map.

Rising in the east, the bright morning sun,
At this lookout point, you'll see clue number one.

Jessa bent her head over the map. Clearly marked was a lookout called "Sunrise Point." She pointed to the map and Rachel nodded. Jessa stood up to go but Rachel stopped her.

"Do you have sugar or juice or whatever you need?"

Jessa felt her cheeks flush with humiliation. *That must have been what Cheryl was saying to Rachel. She must have been briefing her about Jessa's condition.* "Of course," she mumbled and turned and stalked out of the campsite. She jammed her hands into her deep pockets, not only because she was furious, but also to double-check that she had her supplies with her. The deep pockets were another reason she had chosen those particular pirate pants to wear.

Behind her, she could hear Cheryl giggling. "Alicia, I can't keep up with you—wait!"

Jessa looked back. Cheryl's great one-legged costume may have looked good, but there was no way the pirate captain was going to be able to scramble all over the park with one leg tied up. She was hopping around, trying to loosen her leg without taking off her pants. She looked so ridiculous that even in her bad mood, Jessa had to laugh.

"Wait up," Rachel said, bringing the map. "Do you know how to get to the lookout?"

Jessa shook her head. Even though the park was quite close to where she lived, she couldn't remember the last time she had been for a visit. "The map says the trail starts somewhere near the park entrance."

"We're going the wrong way, then. We came in over there." The girls turned around and jogged towards the park office.

"Are you okay? Should you be running?"

"I'm fine," Jessa snapped. "Whatever Cheryl told you, ignore it. I'm perfectly fine and a faster runner than you." She sped up and soon Rachel was panting to keep up. The rhythm of Jessa's steps seemed to say *I'm fine, I'm fine, I'm fine, I'm fine.*

"This must be it."

Jessa and Rachel stood at the lookout. The Gulf Islands rolled one into the other, their edges softened by the haze hanging over the strait. On a clear day Jessa could see all the way to Mount Baker in Washington State, but today, the distant mountain range was invisible.

"So, where's the next clue?"

The girls leaned over the railing, searching the rocky cliff below for signs of another clue. "They wouldn't have put a clue down there," Rachel said.

"I guess not. Look!" A bald eagle soared above them,

followed by two crows. "What are they doing?" Jessa watched as the crows swooped down on the eagle, diving towards him.

"They're picking on him—chasing him!"

It seemed amazing that the crows would bother an eagle so much larger and more formidable than they were. The eagle didn't seem overly bothered by his attackers. He shrugged lazily and banked to the left, gliding out over the trees below and then away over the water until he was lost from sight, the crows in hot pursuit.

"Wow." Jessa stayed where she was, hoping the eagle would return so she could get another look.

"Jessa, we've got to go or we'll never find our treasure. Come on."

Jessa sighed and turned back to the level area of the lookout point. There wasn't much around—a garbage can, a sign pointing to the beach trail, and a bench. "Rising to the east, the bright morning sun," she read from the map. "I know—the bench! You'd probably sit on the bench if you came up here to watch the sunrise."

The girls sat on the bench and looked around. No clue. Rachel walked around the bench, inspecting it carefully, but still couldn't find anything. Jessa kneeled down and looked underneath. She ran her hand under the seat. "I found it!" she said, triumphantly peeling an envelope from its hiding place where it had been taped under the bench.

"Open it!"

"Okay, okay." Jessa fumbled with the envelope and then read aloud,

When searching for clams, you'll need a beach, that's true,
At the northernmost edge, find clue number two.

"The beach!" the girls said together and set off at a

run along the trail leading down to the water.

They slithered to a stop in the loose crunchy mix of sand and crushed seashells on the crescent-shaped beach. "Which way is north?" Jessa asked, momentarily confused. Rachel's eyebrows pushed together.

"On a map, east is on the right." The girls turned so the ocean was on their right. "And north must be that way!" Rachel pointed dead ahead.

It was harder to run in the sand. Jessa's feet sank and twisted away under her and before long her legs ached with the strain of staying upright. Two-thirds of the way down the beach running became impossible as their route was criss-crossed with giant logs and ancient tree stumps that had drifted ashore.

The girls hopped from log to log, their arms out for balance as they tiptoed along the fallen trees.

"We can't go much farther," Rachel said.

A wall of rock faced them at the end of the beach. The cliff towered above them, slick and black, moist from a fine trickle of water that originated somewhere high above them. At the base of the cliff the water pooled and then gurgled down into the ocean in a small stream.

Jessa hopped nimbly over the stream and then followed the base of the cliff until her path was blocked by a giant boulder.

"I can't see another envelope," she said. "Where else could it be?"

Rachel laughed. "Open your eyes! The clue is right in front of you!"

Jessa looked everywhere, and put her hand into several cracks and crevices that marked the face of the massive rock. There was no envelope or piece of paper anywhere that she could see. Rachel laughed louder.

"Where? Show me where!"

"Right in front of your nose!"

"Well, show me!"

Jessa turned around and glared at Rachel. She had known that being Rachel's partner was going to be a problem. Sure enough, Rachel was behaving like a twit. "Show me the envelope!"

"No."

"We're a team! What's wrong with you?"

Rachel couldn't contain herself any longer. She laughed so hard she couldn't speak. She turned Jessa around and pointed at the face of the boulder. There, right in front of their eyes, was the next clue. No wonder Jessa hadn't been able to see an envelope—the message was written in big letters with green chalk.

Hail the great Madrona Tree,
Beneath her roots, clue number three.

Jessa groaned. "This park must have a thousand Madrona trees. How do we know which one is the right one?"

"You looked so funny, trying to find an en . . . en . . . envelope!" Rachel sputtered, still giggling.

"Never mind that. Let's get going." Jessa stalked back along the beach the way they had come. If they were going to have to investigate every Madrona tree in the park, they had no time to waste. This was a task that could take days.

"Wait!" Rachel gasped, running to catch up. "Let's look at the map. They couldn't have meant for us to look at every single possible tree."

The girls unfolded the map and pressed it flat against the broad back of a huge log. The tree had been lying on the beach for so long, it was worn smooth and had turned a pale grey.

"Look!" Rachel jabbed her finger on the map. Someone had drawn a crude picture of a tree close to the other end of the beach. The most prominent part was the root system.

"We must have walked right past it when we left the trail," Jessa said.

Sure enough, close to the end of the beach trail stood an ancient Madrona. Part of the embankment where the tree stood watch had been washed away, revealing about a third of the tree's roots. Tucked inside the tangle of roots was another envelope.

Where climbers climb and eagles soar,
That's where you'll find clue number four.

"Back up to the lookout?" Rachel said doubtfully.

Jessa thought for a moment. "No, I don't think so. Isn't there somewhere around here where people practise mountain climbing? A cliff or some boulders or something?"

"Hey! What clue are you on?"

Jessa jumped, startled to see Cheryl and Alicia barrelling down the hill towards the beach. Jessa shouted out, "We just found number three and we're heading for number four."

"We're just getting number five!" boasted Cheryl. "We would have been closer to the finish if Alicia hadn't been drooling over those mountain climbers."

"What! That's not true—I just wanted to watch that one guy going down the cliff backwards."

"What mountain climbers?" Rachel asked innocently, trying not to seem too interested.

"There's a class or something," Alicia said. "There's a sign posted in the main parking lot—ooof." Cheryl poked her friend in the ribs. "Shhhhh. Don't give them any help!"

"Too late!" grinned Rachel, who sprinted up the trail.

Halfway between the beach and the parking lot, Jessa

slowed to a walk, and then stopped altogether. Rachel disappeared around the bend ahead of her. The tops of the trees turned slowly, and Jessa sat down with a thump, lightheaded and dizzy.

A voice in her head said, "Juice. Drink a juice." Jessa fumbled in her pocket, but her hand felt awkward, as if she were wearing thick gloves. She felt the juice as well as the packet of glucose tablets. She pulled the tablets out of her pocket and tried to peel back the paper. Her fingers refused to cooperate and it was hard to focus her eyes. She hardly noticed when Rachel came slithering to a stop at her side.

"Are you okay?" Rachel sounded panicky. She saw the packet of tablets in Jessa's hands and grabbed them, ripping off the paper as she did.

"Give those back!" Jessa shouted and burst into tears. She felt angry and confused. *Why was Rachel stealing her glucose tablets? Didn't she know she needed them?*

Jessa felt something small and hard in her mouth. She tried to push Rachel's hand away, but Rachel insisted on putting another tablet into Jessa's mouth.

"Chew it! Chew it up!" Rachel said frantically.

Rachel's voice sounded warbly and strange, her words all jumbled. Jessa tasted the sweetness in her mouth and automatically began to chew.

Rachel kept asking something over and over. Jessa tried to concentrate but the effort made her cry harder. "Shut up!" she yelled.

Rachel grabbed Jessa's shoulders and stared into her face. "Do you have juice somewhere?" Rachel insisted.

Numbly, Jessa pulled a juice box from her pocket. Rachel quickly poked the straw into the container and pushed it at Jessa, who turned her head away, her mouth still filled with the crunched-up glucose.

"Drink this!" commanded Rachel, forcing Jessa to take the juice.

Jessa drank, gulping down the whole juice in a few seconds. The sugary tablets washed down as well and Jessa closed her eyes. She felt a little less dizzy now. When she opened her eyes again, she was shocked to see how pale Rachel looked.

"Are you okay?" Rachel asked.

Jessa wiped the tears from her cheeks. Her hand shook. The anger was completely gone now. "I'm sorry," she muttered.

"No kidding," Rachel said. "You scared me half to death! I thought you were going to faint or something. You were all shaky and crying and . . ." Her voice trailed off. "Are you sure you're okay?"

"I'm fine," Jessa said firmly. "I was just having trouble getting the packet of tablets open, that's all." She steadied her voice, determined not to let Rachel see how scared she herself felt. "Thank you for giving me the juice, though I would have been fine in a few minutes."

Rachel didn't look convinced. "I think we should go back to camp."

"No way," Jessa said, getting to her feet. She was feeling better with every passing minute. "I'm fine now. I have another juice in my other pocket. And these." She pulled a plastic sandwich bag from her pocket. When she had left home earlier, it had contained half a dozen crackers. The crackers had since disintegrated into a pile of crumbs.

She opened the bag and scooped out the larger pieces. "Would you like some?" she offered Rachel.

Rachel shook her head. "Errr . . . no thanks. Go ahead."

"I don't blame you," Jessa said, crunching away. She started walking again.

"Are you sure you should—"

"For the last time, I'm fine," Jessa said firmly. "I can

eat this while we're looking for those mountain climbers."

Rachel fell into step beside her. From the worried glances she kept sending Jessa's way, Jessa could tell Rachel was far from reassured. They continued on, silent except for Jessa's crunching of cracker crumbs. By the time they reached the parking lot and found the sign directing people to the climbing area, Jessa was ready to call it quits—not because she felt bad (after her juice and crackers she felt fine) but because it was awful to have to suffer Rachel's pained silence. Every few steps Rachel looked at her like she was checking to see if she was going to go low again. Jessa was amazed to realize she would actually have preferred Rachel's usual snide remarks rather than have to put up with her pity. Being treated like an invalid was infinitely worse than Rachel's usual teasing.

Jessa sighed. Maybe there was some way to get rid of her partner and finish the treasure hunt on her own.

Chapter Nineteen

Jessa soon realized she had little hope of losing her partner, so she tried to ignore Rachel as they searched for the remaining clues.

They found the next one tacked to a "Caution" sign at the base of the climbing boulders.

On the shady side of the great common room,
There you will find some giant mushrooms.
Though brown and not green, they are very much alive,
And under their caps, clue number five.

That sent them hurrying to the rotting log behind the park interpretive centre. Hidden beneath a stubby forest of mushrooms growing next to a fallen cedar tree, they found the next clue.

Kindling and paper, matches and sticks,
Near the heat of the grand fire, there you'll find six.

"I don't think we have to go far," Rachel said with relief. "Isn't that the big fire pit?"

The group picnic area was directly in front of the interpretive centre. The focal point of the group area was a gigantic fire pit.

"Good thing nobody lit a fire in here!" Rachel said. She plucked a clue from where it had been speared on a sharp marshmallow-roasting stick right in the middle of the fire pit.

> *You have nearly come to the end of the trail,*
> *Soon ends the search for your holy grail.*
> *Go to the place where the sand meets the sea,*
> *And there you will find the treasure and me!*

"Back to the beach?"

"Is there only one beach? I didn't see anybody down there. Who are we supposed to meet?"

"Let's look at the map again."

The girls bent over the map. The beach with the boulders and the Madrona tree was clearly marked and easily the largest beach of the park. Along at the south end of the park, near the campground, there was a little cove identified with the words "Sand Beach."

"I bet that's it," Jessa said.

It took nearly fifteen minutes to walk from the interpretive centre, through the campground (the girls noted that their own campsite was completely abandoned), and down the heavily treed path to the small cove and sandy beach they had found on the map.

A colourful sun shelter was plunked in the middle of the beach. Anthony and Bernie, still dressed in their pirate costumes, sat on a large treasure chest. They waved cheerfully when they saw Jessa and Rachel coming towards them.

"Are we the first ones back?" Jessa asked Rachel.

"Maybe . . . who's that?"

Jessa squinted at two figures who seemed to be wading at the water's edge.

"Looks like Cheryl," Jessa said. Her friend's flaming red hair was visible for miles. Cheryl looked up and waved. Then she started jumping up and down, waving her arms.

"What's she saying?" Rachel asked.

Jessa shrugged. It was hard to hear over the breeze and the ocean waves.

"Run! She's telling us to run."

"Why?"

Jessa looked back over her shoulder in time to see Midori and Sarah tearing across the beach towards the shelter. Jessa took off running, determined to beat the other team to the finish line.

The four girls arrived at the sun shelter in a burst of giggles and shrieks.

"First!" Anthony declared, putting his hand on Midori's head. "Second," he said, pointing at Jessa. "Sarah—you're third!" Rachel, having been caught completely by surprise, had been the last to crowd into the shelter.

"I guess your two teams are tied for second place," Bernie said. "Good job, girls. Have a look in the treasure chest for your prizes."

Each girl found a small burlap bag with her name on it in the treasure chest. The others had a mixture of candy and chocolate coins covered with gold foil. Jessa's bag had some diabetic mints, stickers with pictures of horses, and a pencil with a horse-head eraser stuck on the end.

"Who's still missing?" Anthony asked.

"Bridget and Monika," Rachel said quickly.

"What took you guys so long?" Cheryl asked, joining the others in the shelter. "We've been back for three hours!"

"Try three minutes!" laughed Anthony, ignoring his sister's glare.

"Why don't you all hang out down by the water and look for starfish or something while we wait for the last two."

"Starfish?" Jessa asked.

"You should see some of them. They're huge and bright purple!" Cheryl said, as she headed back down towards the water followed by the rest of the girls. Everyone pulled off their shoes and socks and paddled in the shallows, searching for starfish, urchins, and small fish.

About twenty minutes later, Bernie strolled down to join them. She had her hands shoved deep into her pockets and kept scanning the beach back towards the path.

"I think maybe we should go and look for them," she said, unable to disguise the worry in her voice.

Rachel looked up sharply. "Do you think they got lost?"

Jessa couldn't see how anyone could get lost on the clearly marked trails of the park. On the other hand, Monika was famous for her thrill-seeking personality. Maybe she had decided to tackle the rock-climbing boulders and had fallen and hit her head. Maybe even as the rest of them were playing in the water, she was lying unconscious in a pool of blood!

"Someone has to stay here," said Anthony, joining the others who were now huddled together around Bernie. "Jessa and Rachel? Can you stay here at the beach in case they show up? Bernie and I know where the clues would have led them. Cheryl and Midori—can you go back to our campsite in case they show up there? And Alicia and Sarah—you two could maybe head for the other beach in case they had trouble reading their map."

"Are there bears in this park?" Cheryl asked, her eyes wide with horror.

Jessa's mental picture of the fallen Monika now included a salivating bear drooling over the bloody remains of her friend. She shuddered.

"Yeah, big grizzlies. Huge, hungry, crazed grizzlies,"

Anthony said, grinning wickedly. But his joking seemed half-hearted, as if he were really worried.

Bernie kicked at his shins. "This is no time for teasing," she said firmly. "No. There are no bears here. Come on—let's get going. We'll all meet back here in half an hour, with or without them. If they haven't shown up by then, we'll have to call in the park rangers."

Everyone hurried to find their shoes and then scurried off to their destinations, chins set and suddenly very quiet.

Jessa and Rachel made their way back to the shelter and sat side by side on the big treasure chest. For a few minutes, neither of them said anything. Looking out over the glittering water, the sun dancing off the ripples, it seemed impossible that something nasty could have happened to their friends.

"What if one of them slipped on the trail going down to the other beach?" Rachel said. "It was kind of steep in places."

"But why wouldn't the other one have come for help?"

"Maybe she tried to climb down to help and fell, too."

"Maybe." A terrible thought occurred to Jessa. "I know Bernie said there aren't any bears here, but I know for sure there are cougars."

Rachel made a horrified choking noise. "You're right. Remember last summer when that girl was pulled off her horse by that starving cougar and needed 147 stitches to close up the gashes?"

Jessa shuddered. "The cougar practically ripped her arm off. I remember." She swallowed hard and chewed on the inside of her cheek. The pictures in her head were getting more and more hideous by the moment. Now poor Monika was lying in a pool of blood with a ravenous cougar perched on her chest!

She snapped herself out of it. "We have to think about something else. They're probably fine."

"Okay," Rachel said. "What if there's some psycho guy with an axe running around looking for victims. . . ."

"Shut up!" Jessa punched Rachel's arm. "You're freaking me out." Jessa kept craning her neck to look back over her shoulder. She sure didn't want anyone or anything sneaking up on her. She wished now she had been one of the girls who was out looking rather than having to sit still waiting for something to happen.

"Monika!" Rachel screeched. Jessa nearly jumped out of her skin. She turned around to face the beach and saw the strangest thing. Monika was wading along knee deep in the water, and just beyond her, someone was paddling a double kayak.

"Ahoy!" Monika yelled.

"Where's Bridget?" Jessa asked.

"Is that her in the front of the kayak?" Rachel asked. Both girls were already on their feet and running down towards the water.

As they drew closer they could see that the person in the front of the kayak was indeed Bridget. Bridget raised her paddle in the air. Water droplets glinted in the bright sunshine as they fell from her paddle tip.

"What are you doing out there?" Rachel yelled.

Jessa pushed back her eye patch so she could see better.

"We went to the wrong beach."

The kayak nosed up through the shallows and crunched gently into the sand at Jessa's feet. The person in the back of the kayak was Blake Ryerson. He looked more than a little uncomfortable being scrutinized by Jessa and Rachel.

"Hi, Blake," Rachel said. "Where did you come from?"

"We're camped around on the other side of the point—in the camping area for kayakers."

"We were stuck over there on the other beach, and we didn't feel like walking all the way around on the trail," explained Monika, drying her feet and putting on her socks and shoes.

"The tide came up so we couldn't walk around the point to get from that beach to this one without getting wet," Bridget added. Then she looked a bit embarrassed. "Well, I didn't get wet—Blake came by and gave me a lift. Monika walked beside us."

Bridget climbed out of the front cockpit and carefully tucked the spray skirt and life jacket away. With Blake's help, she secured the paddle to the top of the kayak.

"You can paddle that thing by yourself?" Rachel asked.

"He was in it by himself when we saw him," Monika said.

Blake levered his paddle against the sand and eased himself backwards out into deeper water. He didn't say a word as he swung the kayak around so he was facing the way he had come and then paddled off, leaving all four girls standing on the beach.

"Does he know how to talk?" Rachel asked.

"Sure he does," defended Monika. "He's just shy. Blake and Bridget are the perfect match."

"Oooooh," Rachel teased. "I noticed Bridget was the one in the kayak."

"That was just because I know how to paddle," Bridget said softly.

"Oh, sure," Rachel said.

Jessa watched Blake paddle around the point and out of sight. She felt slightly guilty about not protecting Bridget from Rachel's teasing. Jessa knew well enough what it felt like to be picked on.

"Hey!" The girls turned around to see Anthony and Bernie jogging across the sand towards them. "Where the heck did you come from?"

"We took the local ferry service," quipped Monika.

"They ran into a friend who has a kayak over on the other beach," explained Rachel, in answer to Anthony's raised eyebrows.

"Your friend wouldn't be called Blake?"

It was Monika's turn to look confused. "How did you know his name?"

"While we were running around like fools looking for you, we went over to the kayak campers. They were missing their son. We didn't realize you had shanghaied him and his vessel."

"Well, he's on his way back now," said Rachel.

"You're alive!" squealed Cheryl, who pelted across the beach to join them. The other three girls followed close behind. Monika had to tell the whole story all over again for their benefit.

"Girls!" Anthony said. "Shhhhh! Listen up for a minute. It's nearly dinner time and Jessa, for one, has to eat on time."

The festive mood of the happy reunion dampened as everyone looked at Jessa. "We'd better get going," Rachel said. "Jessa gets out of control when she's low."

Jessa felt her cheeks flush. At that moment she hated Rachel more than anyone else on the planet. There was no reason to humiliate her in front of all her friends. She turned away from the group and walked back towards the campsite, alone.

Chapter Twenty

Back at camp the girls flew into a frenzy of activity. Bridget and Sarah helped Anthony get the fire going to roast hot dogs. Bernie helped Monika and Rachel erect another tent. Midori and Cheryl organized sleeping bags in their tent and Jessa and Alicia were given the job of filling all the water containers at the nearby tap and bringing them back to camp.

When the hot dogs were cooking, Cheryl asked, "Do you have to test your blood or something?"

Jessa glared at her friend. Of course she had to do a blood test. She just didn't feel like doing it in front of everyone like she was in some kind of freak show.

"I'm going to do it in the tent."

"Can I watch?" Monika asked.

Before Jessa could answer, Rachel said, "Leave her alone. This isn't a circus sideshow."

For a moment, Jessa met Rachel's gaze. Then she ducked into the tent and zipped shut the front and back flaps. Outside she could hear the pop and crackle of the fire. The hot dogs sizzled and spit, and every now and then Anthony exclaimed, "Ouch!" or "Away with you, evil smoke!" She could also hear her friends talking softly.

"It's so gross, having shots every day." Monika sounded appalled.

"She has to have them two or three times and test her

blood more than that," Cheryl said.

"Yuck. I couldn't do it," said Sarah.

"You would do it, because if you didn't you'd get very sick and maybe even die," Rachel retorted.

Jessa poked her finger with the sharp lancet. A large drop of blood welled up on her finger tip. She touched it to the end of the blood glucose strip and her machine beeped.

It was bizarre listening to her friends talk about her as if she weren't there.

"You should have seen her today when she had an insulin reaction," said Rachel, dropping her voice so low Jessa had to strain to hear. "She started crying and nearly bit my head off when I made her drink some juice. It was really lucky I was there. I probably saved her life."

In the tent, Jessa rolled her eyes. She couldn't stand the sound of Rachel's inflated sense of self-importance. It hadn't been that bad. *She would have been fine as soon as she had eaten the glucose. Why was everyone making such a big deal out of everything?* Her tester beeped and Jessa read the number: 14.4. That was high so she drew up a little extra insulin in a syringe. She gave herself the shot in her thigh and then emerged back out into the campsite.

The other girls fell silent as she walked over to the fire and stood beside Anthony.

"Looks good," she said, ignoring them all.

"Hungry?" he asked.

"Yup!" she said, patting her tummy.

"There are some potato chips on the table, if you'd like to get started."

Jessa counted ten chips onto her plate. She knew that was about one starch choice. In her head she quickly calculated that she could also eat two hot dogs and drink a glass of juice without disrupting her meal plan.

She was relieved to hear Rachel launching in on another round of teasing directed at poor Bridget—about how she had been swept off her feet by a passing yachtsman.

In the hubbub of chatter and waves of laughter, nobody seemed to notice how quiet Jessa had become.

"So, how was the party, darling?" Granny asked.

Jessa stared out the car window, trying to make out the forms of trees in the heavy black shadows outside.

"Fine. I got some good presents. Rachel gave me a really nice horse book."

Jessa brooded in silence for the rest of the ride home. The truth was she had found the party exhausting. It had been impossible to just relax and enjoy the dumb games Bernie and Anthony had arranged. The ghost stories had seemed lame and Rachel had insisted on asking her how she was feeling every fifteen minutes. She wished she hadn't bothered with a birthday party at all.

Romeo greeted her at the front door with a big slurpy lick and much tail-wagging. He trotted up the stairs close on her heels and hopped neatly onto the bed. He whined and tipped his head from side to side, wondering why his mistress was sitting at her desk instead of joining him. Jessa opened her journal.

Dear Diary,

It is nearly midnight and I don't want to go to bed. I didn't think I would have a lousy time at the birthday party but that's what happened. Everybody thinks I'm weird or that I'm about to faint or something. In my head I keep hearing the question "Why me? Why me? Why me?" What did I do wrong to get punished with having stupid diabetes? Why isn't there a cure? Why do I have to have shots every day for the rest of my life? Why do I have to feel so horrible when I go low? Why? Why? Why?

She threw her pen across the room and flung herself on the bed. Her shoulders heaved with each wracking sob. Romeo crept alongside her and licked at the salty tears on her cheeks. Despite herself, she grinned. "Stop it, you twerpy dog." Romeo paid no attention. He wriggled and licked and squirmed to be closer to her. The more she tried to push him away, the more he thought they were playing some sort of game.

"Romeo, stop!" By now Jessa was giggling and sniffling in a confused jumble of gasps and sobs. It was simply impossible to be miserable with Romeo's front paws planted on her chest, his doggy breath in her face.

She wrapped her arms around his white ruff and pulled him close. "You stupid dog," she said, burying her face in his soft fur. "Lie still so we can get some sleep."

Romeo seemed to understand. He lay down beside Jessa and stretched his chin out on her pillow. With her hand resting on his head, Jessa soon fell into a deep and dreamless sleep.

"Jessa? Mrs. Bailey's on the phone." Granny's voice was loud in the small room.

Jessa dragged herself out of bed. Romeo had already disappeared. Sunlight streamed in through her bedroom window. She staggered downstairs.

"Hello?"

"Morning, Jessa." Mrs. Bailey was her usual gruff and businesslike self. "I thought you might like to know that Molly won't be out for the next couple of days, so if you'd like to come and ride Rebel that would be fine. When would you like to have another lesson on Jasmine? And I don't mean to rush you, dear, but when do you think you'll be able to get back to your regular days of cleaning stalls?"

Jessa's body might have been standing upright holding the phone to her ear, but her brain was still half asleep. "Ride Rebel?" That sounded like a good idea. "Okay. I can come out today and do some stalls. I feel fine."

"And Jasmine?"

Jessa sighed. Her last lesson had been such a disaster she wasn't exactly thrilled with the prospect of being humiliated again. She'd had about enough humiliation recently to last her a lifetime.

"Well? That horse needs to be ridden. As far as I'm concerned, the quicker you learn to get along with her, the better."

"Okay. How about the day after tomorrow?"

"Perfect. Molly should be back by then. One o'clock sound good to you?"

It didn't sound good at all, but Jessa didn't say that. Instead, she agreed to the plan and hung up the phone with a thunk.

"Going to the barn, I presume?" her grandmother asked.

"Yes." Jessa decided against going back to the park— she had "celebrated" her birthday enough.

"Where's Mom?"

"At work."

"Oh, right. I forgot." Jessa's mother worked at various offices and businesses as a book-keeper. She also took correspondence courses and night classes because she wanted to become an accountant.

"I have the car. I dropped your mother off so I'd be

166

able to give you a ride, if you like. Your mother thought that might be better than riding your bike to the barn all alone."

Jessa gritted her teeth. "Granny," she said. "I am not a baby. I can ride my bike just like I usually do."

Jessa and her grandmother faced each other in the kitchen. "It takes five minutes for me to get there. I'll be fine." Jessa fully expected a battle, but her grandmother didn't argue.

"You're right. You're certainly not a baby, though you'll always seem like it to me!" She kissed Jessa on the forehead. "So, blood test, shot, and then a balanced breakfast, right?" Granny had obviously memorized her instructions.

"Right," said Jessa. As much as she despised her new routine, there was no point in making trouble over it. At least she could ride her bike. That was worth something.

Jessa and Romeo had only been at the barn for fifteen minutes when Cheryl popped her head into Brandy's stall and said, "Need a hand in there?"

"You look awful!" exclaimed Jessa.

"Yeah, well, you're probably the only one of the whole party who got any sleep last night. I can't believe I actually had a fight with my mother about coming to the barn. For a change, I was the one who didn't want to come."

"Why didn't you just take a day off?"

"I've already taken a few days off with the party and everything. My mom said that agreeing to ride Billy Jack regularly was a big responsibility and I couldn't just skip day after day because I was a bit tired."

Jessa thought Cheryl looked more than a "bit" tired. Her blazing red hair stood straight up in the back and her skin looked paler than usual. To her credit, Cheryl didn't press Jessa about why she hadn't come back to the party in the morning. It had been pretty obvious Jessa was having a miserable time.

"So, do you want a hand or what?"

"Sure. Do you want to go on a trail ride with me?"

Cheryl nodded and for a moment, Jessa forgot that her life was any different than it had ever been. She scraped the rest of the damp bedding out with a shovel and tossed it into the wheelbarrow. It was strange how comforting she found the familiar rhythm of cleaning stalls, putting in fresh bedding, filling water buckets, and tossing hay bales from the loft.

Working side by side with Cheryl made the whole process rather entertaining. Despite her lack of sleep, her friend's stream of chatter never slowed. Jessa found herself being regaled by stories of the camp-out.

"So then at about one in the morning, Rachel and Monika decided to raid the kayakers' tents. Blake was there with his dad and about five other boys and Monika came up with this crazy idea of hiding their frying pan."

"Their frying pan? Why?"

"So they wouldn't be able to cook pancakes at breakfast. You know, as a kind of practical joke."

It sounded like a dumb joke to Jessa but she didn't say anything. Instead, she concentrated on scrubbing out Jasmine's water bucket.

"Anyway, they were getting all ready to go with their flashlights and emergency food supplies—"

"What!"

"Rachel thought it was possible they might get lost and she didn't want to starve to death. They were just arguing about whether they should take a sleeping bag in case they needed to keep warm while they were lost when we heard this animal growling outside the tents."

"Really? What kind of animal?"

"We didn't know and we were all piled into Rachel and Monika's tent and we were totally scared because we thought maybe it was a bear or a wolf or something."

"There are no bears or wolves near Victoria."

"Or a cougar or even a crazed dog. Anyway, we had no idea what it was and then we saw this shadow moving closer to our tent and Midori was hiding under her sleeping bag and I thought Sarah was going to cry and we were sitting there in the dark with the flashlight going dimmer and dimmer and then we saw another shadow. . . ."

Cheryl was breathing hard, as if she were reliving the terror from the night before. "So then I screamed and that made everyone else scream and Anthony came tearing out of his tent with his big flashlight and we heard lots of yelling and running feet so we all piled out of the tent and guess what?"

"What?"

"It was Blake and two of his friends playing a trick on us! We were so wide awake that Anthony said we should all have some hot chocolate, but then Blake and the other boys decided his father would get worried if he found out they weren't in their tents so they left right away. Blake can talk, you know."

"I know that. I've heard him giving answers in class."

"No, I mean, he's actually quite nice. Just very shy. His friends were the ones who convinced him to sneak over to our campsite. I think Bridget likes him a lot."

"They can go on a kayaking trip for their honeymoon," Jessa joked.

With the two of them working and chattering away, it took no time at all to clean the stalls. As soon as they were done the girls retrieved their horses from the paddocks and fastened them in the cross-ties. Jessa hummed softly under her breath as she whisked a stiff brush over Rebel's withers.

She tacked up, carefully checked to see that she had plenty of juice and crackers in her backpack, and then mounted. Cheryl was ready a moment later and the two girls set off down the driveway together, Romeo trotting obediently behind them.

Jessa couldn't think of anywhere she would rather be. She reached forward and gave Rebel a resounding pat on the neck. He responded to her temporary lack of rein contact by snatching a mouthful of grass. "Some things never change," she remarked with a grin.

Chapter Twenty-one

"Jessa! What the heck are you doing up there?" Mrs. Bailey sounded as exasperated as Jessa felt.

"She won't do it!"

"Don't slouch like that! Sit up straight and ask again."

Jessa gathered her reins, pushed Jasmine forward with a firm leg, and tried to collect Jasmine's walk.

"Half-halt . . . good, now ask—she can do this in her sleep."

Jessa slid her outside leg back. The mare's broad side seemed vast compared to Rebel's. Asking her pony to canter was easy—she only needed to move her leg the tiniest bit and he hopped eagerly forward. Jasmine was another story entirely. Not only was she huge, she moved more slowly than the quicker pony. She wasn't sluggish, but seemed thoughtful and determined to get her rider to do everything exactly right.

"Canter," Jessa said brightly, hoping the voice aid would help.

Beneath her, Jasmine felt like she was lifting up, tipping backwards onto her haunches as she gathered herself to make the upward transition from walk to canter.

"There you go! Keep your leg on—leg on!"

Though Mrs. Bailey's voice was loud and insistent, after two canter strides Jasmine fell back into a trot.

"You can't let your legs flop around like that. You have to keep contact with her! And don't hold her back once she's moving forward. Your hands have to follow the motion of her head and neck."

Jessa had heard it all before, but for some reason even the simplest exercises were a major challenge on Mrs. Bailey's super-horse. Jessa pulled her up and walked over to Mrs. Bailey.

"Jasmine, baby. What are you doing? Giving poor Jessa a hard time? Mumsy can't ride you at the moment. . . ."

Mrs. Bailey winked up at Jessa from under her cowboy hat. "You're doing fine. You're going to have to develop a more effective leg to ride her well."

"I could just ride Rebel again . . . my leg's good enough. . . ."

Mrs. Bailey silenced her pupil with a sweep of her hand. "Good enough for your pony, perhaps, but if you keep riding him you will never get any better. It's up to you, of course. If you honestly feel this horse can't teach you anything, by all means, go back to riding Rebel. Molly will have to find herself another pony."

Jessa reached forward and stroked Jasmine's long, glossy neck. She knew that what Mrs. Bailey was saying was true. Jasmine could do it all, if only Jessa could figure out how to ask her.

"Ready to try the canter again?"

"I guess so."

"Don't sound so happy!"

Jessa managed a half smile. "Come on, Jasmine. Let's go."

"Now remember, legs, legs, legs . . . no! That doesn't mean pull up your knees! Stretch your legs long . . . long. Drop your stirrups!"

Jessa ignored the little knot of fear in her chest. Ride without stirrups? It was a long way down if she fell off.

"Cross them over her withers—that's it."

Surely Mrs. Bailey wasn't going to ask her to try to canter without stirrups?

"Effective legs don't mean pinching with your knees! Now, lower legs on and ask her to come forward into the bit. Good! That's a better walk. Now, half-halt and ask for the C-A-N-T-E-R."

Mrs. Bailey spelled the word so Jasmine wouldn't recognize the voice command.

Looking straight ahead and raising her chin, Jessa asked for the canter. Jasmine lifted herself straight into the canter and under her breath, Jessa chanted to the rhythm of the mare's big stride, "Keep the leg on, keep the leg on."

"Much better!" Mrs. Bailey shouted. "Keep going all the way around the ring! Don't tip forward! Following hands, following hands—much better!"

Sitting deep in the saddle Jessa was astounded at the power and grace of Jasmine's canter. She had heard of horses who felt like a rocking horse, but she'd never experienced anything quite like this. The controlled power was incredible and she couldn't help smiling as they passed the gate to the riding ring without breaking stride.

"And sit deep, come back to sitting trot. Good. Now, keep the energy of the canter and show me a good trot."

The downward transition felt rather bumpy but Jasmine quickly settled into a very forward, lively trot.

"Now you two are waking up! Much, much better, Jessa."

By the end of the riding lesson, the rest of which Mrs. Bailey insisted on conducting without stirrups, Jessa's legs felt like rubber. When she leaped off Jasmine, her knees sagged when she hit the ground.

"Jessa! That was a huge improvement from last time.

How did you feel up there?"

"Pretty good at the end," Jessa had to admit. She pulled the reins over Jasmine's head and rubbed her mount's forehead.

"Patience—that's all you need with her. And lots of practice. When can you ride her again?"

Jessa pushed her eyebrows together.

"Don't worry, dear. You can clean stalls an extra day a week to cover the costs of a few extra lessons. Molly will be paying for her rides on Rebel which will help with expenses around here."

It was as if Mrs. Bailey had read her mind. There was no way her mom could afford to lease a horse like Jasmine. Jessa also now understood why Molly didn't seem to be mucking out stalls.

"And you're doing me a favour by riding her regularly. If you can get up to speed you'll be keeping her in good shape for me. I simply can't ride as much or as hard as I used to. And I don't want just anyone riding her."

Jessa patted the chestnut mare on the neck. She knew full well what an honour it was to be riding Mrs. Bailey's baby. Walter ambled over to stand beside Mrs. Bailey.

"You ride her better than you think," he said, winking at Jessa.

Despite the encouragement, Jessa still wondered whether she wouldn't be better off sticking with Rebel—at least for the next year or so. But then Jasmine gave her a friendly push in the side and Jessa decided to keep her doubts to herself. Silently, she hoped that she wouldn't make too big a fool of herself, or that she wouldn't fall off and get badly injured. No matter what Mrs. Bailey said about her horse being gentle, wise, and sensible, Jasmine was a very big girl and even the gentlest tumble meant a very long fall.

Chapter Twenty-two

At first Jessa thought the knocking was part of her dream. She was back in her hospital bed in Calgary and a nurse was trying to come into her room to tell her that there had been a mistake, that Jessa wasn't really a diabetic after all.

Jessa rolled over and watched the nurse come into her room. The nurse's hands were green and stringy, like spinach pasta.

"I've brought you something," the nurse said.

Jessa sat up in the hospital room and started riding her chair around and around in small circles. The chair bucked and kicked and Jessa wrapped her arms around the chair back so she didn't fall off.

"Are you awake yet?"

The knocking was louder now. "Jessa?? Are you okay in there?"

The dream chair softened into a pillow. "I'm fine. What?"

"Don't sound so grumpy," her mother said, coming into the bedroom. "I have good news for you."

"Last time you said that you told me I was going to go on a trail ride in the mountains," Jessa said glumly.

"Well, guess what? You're going on a trail ride in the Rocky Mountains."

"Yeah, right." Sometimes her mother's sense of humour was so un-funny it wasn't funny. "Let me go back to sleep."

"I'm serious. I just got off the phone with Bill from Flannigan's and we've arranged everything. You fly out on Sunday. Granny will take you over on the ferry and drop you off at the airport. It's time for her to head back to Vancouver anyway. I think we're managing fine, don't you?"

"What?" Somehow, her mother's words were all blurred together and Jessa couldn't figure out what she was saying. Another trail ride? Granny going back to Vancouver? "What?" she repeated, her head still thick with sleep.

"Apparently there's a father and his little boy who are going on next week's trail ride. The son is also a diabetic and his father is a doctor. When Bill took their reservation he told them about you, then he called me. It was the doctor's idea you try again."

"The boy is a diabetic?"

"He's quite young—only six. He was diagnosed two years ago."

Romeo shifted at the bottom of the bed, then tucked his nose back under the white tip of his tail and went back to sleep.

"You two," her mother laughed. "You'd sleep all day if I'd let you!"

"I'm awake now!" Jessa said, an edge of excitement creeping into her voice. "Do you really think I should go?"

"Of course you should go!" Granny stepped into the bedroom to join them. "Why on earth wouldn't you?"

Needles. Blood tests. Going low. Fainting. Dropping her insulin bottle off a cliff. Jessa could think of a thousand reasons why she shouldn't go.

Jessa's mother was not so pessimistic. "With your own private doctor to supervise, someone whose own child is a diabetic—well, I agree one hundred per cent with Granny. I think you'll have a marvellous time."

With her mother and grandmother beaming at her so triumphantly, Jessa could hardly disagree. What they said about having a doctor close by was true, but that didn't stop the gnawing anxiety inside her that was growing stronger by the minute. At the same time, the thought of going back to the mountains was so exciting she could hardly wait. It felt like there was a whole war of feelings going on, and the more she thought about going on the trip, the louder the battle raged.

"Couldn't you come with me?" she asked her mother two days later at breakfast.

"I thought about it, actually. But I've already taken more time off work than I should have and really, as your grandmother keeps reminding me, it's important that you find your feet. Once you get there and climb on a horse, you'll feel fine. I know you."

I know you. There were few words that irritated her more. *Her mother didn't have the foggiest idea how she felt. No one did.*

The more Jessa thought about her impending departure, the more she didn't want to go. *How was she supposed to talk to a complete stranger about how she was feeling? The doctor was supposed to be going on vacation. Why would he want to be bothered with a patient he didn't even know?* Jessa didn't want to face Bill or anyone else from Flannigan's. She had already caused more than enough trouble and ruined one trail ride for everyone.

Neither her mother nor her grandmother seemed the least bit concerned. Granny had been merrily packing ever since the trip had been arranged. "Don't misunderstand me, dear—I have had a wonderful time visiting you. But I'm looking forward to getting back to my own place. My garden is probably completely overgrown!"

Jessa doubted it. Granny hadn't been in Kenwood for

that long.

"Ready to go to the barn? What's up? This is your last chance to ride before you leave tomorrow."

Nobody had to tell her. *What had happened to the fun-filled summer she had planned?* Riding Jasmine was so far from being a resounding success, Jessa could hardly muster any enthusiasm. Molly was going to be riding Rebel so she wouldn't even be able to say a private goodbye to her beloved pony—say goodbye to leave for a trip she wasn't even sure she wanted to take.

"Are you okay!?"

Jessa looked up at two faces staring down at her where she lay in the dirt. Mrs. Bailey looked worried. Jasmine looked a little surprised. She stretched her nose down towards Jessa as if to ask what her rider was doing lying on the ground. Though Jessa's mouth opened and shut, no sound came out and her eyes watered as she fought unbelievable pain. She felt like she had been skewered to the ground with a spear rammed right through her chest.

"It's all right, dear. You've knocked the wind out of yourself. Try to relax and breathe."

All Jessa could manage at first was a tiny sip of air. The band around her chest tightened and her heart pounded wildly.

"That's it, breathe in . . . and again. . . ."

Jessa struggled to draw in a small breath.

"Ohhh," Jessa moaned. Mrs. Bailey helped her sit up, so that Jessa's legs stuck straight out in front of her.

Mrs. Bailey rubbed Jessa's back and said, "Your approach was totally crooked. No wonder she stopped like that. Here, give me your hand." They both groaned as Jessa pulled herself to her feet. "You want to try that again?"

Jessa shook her head firmly, still gasping a little. *No*

way. She had tried to tell Mrs. Bailey she wasn't ready for cross-poles on Jasmine, but the older woman had ignored her protests. The reassurances that Jessa was riding well and that Jasmine could jump cross-poles with one leg tied up had done nothing to ease Jessa's nerves.

"Too bad. You're not hurt and you have to show her you know what you're doing. I'd get on myself, but my backside is still a bit sore."

The next thing Jessa knew she was back in the saddle, finding her stirrups with her toes. She straightened her helmet and picked up her reins.

"Right, off you go. Circle at the trot a couple of times, find your rhythm. Then pick up a canter between K and C and then try this line again."

Mrs. Bailey clucked from the ground and Jasmine picked up the trot without any encouragement from Jessa. "Leg on, that's it!"

There was no chance to be afraid. If Jessa didn't pay attention, she was going to fall off again before they got anywhere near a fence.

"That's good . . . now canter—and get organized up there, shorten your reins. . . ."

A moment later Jessa and Jasmine cantered easily towards the first fence. Jessa readied herself but this time didn't get ahead of the jump. Jasmine popped over neatly, fitted in three canter strides, and took the second jump easily.

"Bravo!" shouted Mrs. Bailey. "Back to the trot now and you can cool her out. Always best to end on a good note. Excellent, Jessa! I knew you could do it."

Jessa reached forward and gave the chestnut mare a resounding pat on the neck. "Good girl, Jasmine," she said. She had never felt anything quite like it before. They may have been only small cross-pole jumps, but when Jasmine jumped it felt like Jessa was soaring. For once, she was sorry her lesson was over. She would have loved to keep on going forever.

Chapter Twenty-three

It was the clear, biting quality of the air that hit Jessa first as she jumped out of the van in the parking lot at Flannigan's Lodge. This time she was the last to arrive. The rest of the guests were already down near the corrals with the horses.

"Welcome back, Jessa," grinned Bing, her hands on her hips. "Didn't give me a chance to say goodbye last time! Here, take this on down to your horse."

The cook reached into a white pail and pulled out a fat carrot. "Who is my horse?" Jessa asked Bill.

"Would you like to ride Spirit again?"

"Sure!"

"Come on, then. It'll be dark before long."

So far, the best part about the trip was that ever since she had arrived at the Calgary airport, Bill had talked about nothing but horses, some of the more memorable city slickers who had visited over the summer, and how he was noticing a chill in the air late at night that he swore carried the whiff of snow. Never once did he mention diabetes. Jessa could have kissed his stubbly cheek for that.

"Do you think it might snow up at Skoki Lake camp?"

Bill's long, easy stride ate up the ground between the lodge and the corrals. Jessa had to jog to keep up.

"Could happen," he drawled. "Wouldn't be the first

time. That's the risk you take during the last couple of trips each season. Here's someone I'd like you to meet."

He stopped at the hitching rail where several guests were brushing their horses and getting acquainted.

"Al?"

A man Jessa hadn't even noticed stepped out from behind a squat black horse. The doctor was very short, about the same size as Jessa, and skinny as a toothpick. He was completely bald and his smooth, shiny head glowed in the late afternoon sun. "Jessa, this is Dr. Miller," Bill said.

"Call me Alvin. Al for short. Pleased to meet you, Jessa."

Jessa nodded and shook hands when he offered. She didn't think she had ever called a doctor by his first name before. Then again, she had never met a doctor who wore a checkered shirt, cut-off shorts, and a pair of cowboy boots, either. The boots were fascinating—made of some kind of cherry red leather. His knobby knees reminded her of the knotted lumps of bird legs. She couldn't help but smile when he reached behind his horse and pulled a little boy into view.

"This is my son, Ryan."

There was no need for an introduction. The little boy looked like a miniature clone of his dad. He was tiny and wore a checkered shirt, shorts, and red cowboy boots.

"Hi," Jessa said. Ryan stepped sideways and hid behind his father's skinny legs.

"He's a bit shy," Dr. Miller said. "I understand you are quite a horsewoman?"

Jessa blushed. "I have a . . ." she stopped herself. "I ride a couple of different horses at home. My pony's name is Rebel. And I've just started riding a new mare called Jasmine."

The doctor looked impressed.

"I started riding on my father's ranch when I was Ryan's age! But it's been years since I sat in a saddle. You can give me a few tips."

"Who are you riding, Ryan?"

"Stardust."

Behind the doctor's horse stood a flea-bitten grey pony. "He's gorgeous. Do you need a hand grooming him?"

Ryan bobbed his head and silently handed Jessa a brush.

"Come on," she said, and he followed her obediently to Stardust's side.

"Have you been riding before?"

"Uh-huh."

Ryan nodded and watched everything Jessa did. He copied her exactly, whisking the dandy brush over his pony's shoulder with a professional flick of his wrist.

"I'll leave you here," Bill said, nodding over the pony's back. "I'll be back up at the lodge. If you want to catch Spirit and give him a quick grooming, that would be fine."

Jessa nodded in reply. She watched the little boy carefully brushing his pony. He seemed so normal. It seemed hard to believe he was also a diabetic, though she wasn't sure exactly why she thought he would behave somehow differently from any other six-year-old boy.

"I'll show you how to pick up his feet," Jessa offered. "And when we've finished with your pony, you could help me groom my horse, if you like. His name is Spirit."

The boy nodded again. Jessa remembered the carrot in her back pocket and she grabbed it and snapped it in half. The pony craned his head around to see what treat was in store for him.

"Hold it like this—so it's pointing into his mouth . . . good."

Ryan laughed as Stardust crunched away noisily. "He likes that!"

"Carrots are candy for horses," Jessa said.

"Candy for horses," her smaller friend repeated.

In bed in the lodge that night, Jessa stared at the red light of the little monitor standing on her bedside table. It was very, very strange to know that the other end of the baby monitor was set up in the doctor's room. "Just in case you have a problem during the night," he had grinned with a wink over dinner. That was about the extent of the discussion. Blood tests and shots were just part of the routine for Ryan and his father. It was over so quickly and with so little fuss that the other guests hardly noticed what was happening.

Just before the dinner shot, Dr. Miller had quickly and efficiently asked Jessa about her insulin dose, number of shots a day, and her diet. After that, though Jessa had the distinct impression the doctor was keeping an eye on her, he didn't bother her at all. It was strange to be looking after everything by herself, but a big relief to know he was there in case she needed advice or help.

Strangely, the glowing red light of the monitor didn't upset her, didn't feel like an invasion of privacy. Knowing the doctor was at the other end made her feel safe and protected. In the dark, she gave the monitor a friendly wave. Then she sighed, rolled over, and fell fast asleep.

"Look up!" Russ shouted, pointing far above.

The six guests on the trip all looked up. Far above them, a large bird floated across a piercing blue backdrop.

"What is that?" Dr. Miller asked. "That's not an eagle, is it?"

"Osprey," answered Russ.

The underside of the majestic bird was dark brown and white. The tips of the bird's long flight feathers looked like fingertips brushing the sky.

"They're fantastic at fishing! The soles of their feet are very scaly to help them hold onto slippery fish. If you're lucky, you'll get to see one diving into the lake."

The bird disappeared over a rise and Jessa felt a stab of disappointment when she could no longer see him. It was the second day of the trip and getting close to lunchtime and their arrival at the Skoki Lake camp.

This trip was so different from the first one. Everything seemed new, and yet familiar. What was most amazing was how much she remembered from earlier in the summer. The mountains still reared up and surrounded her no matter which way she looked. The air was filled with a kind of drama even when nothing in particular was happening.

This time, though, she could enjoy all the rich details of the high mountain valleys because she felt quite normal. Healthy. It struck her as strange that never before had she felt grateful for simply feeling okay.

"Who's ready for lunch?" Russell called from the head of the line.

There was a chorus of agreement. Riding in the mountains, no matter how big the pancake breakfast, gave everyone a vigorous appetite.

"Doing okay, Jessa?"

Ryan was looking back over his shoulder. He had specially asked for Jessa to be behind him in the line and had totally gotten over his initial shyness.

"I'm fine—how about you?"

"Great!" he grinned.

Even though he was so much younger, Jessa had found he was great company.

"Russ said we could have either peanut butter or

cheese sandwiches," he said. Somehow he always knew what was going to be offered for the next meal. "I'm going to have peanut butter. What are you going to have?"

"Same as you. Do you want to sit together?"

Ryan grinned again and once the horses had been tethered for lunch, he joined Jessa in the lineup for lunch. Thick slabs of fresh bread slathered with peanut butter and sugar-free jam never tasted so good.

"Do you want to sit up by the water?" Jessa asked.

"Can we, Dad?"

"Just be careful you don't fall in! That water is extremely cold!"

The two kids clambered up over rocks and boulders until they were right at the edge of Skoki Lake. The water was a strange shade of greeny blue.

"It looks like somebody painted it," Jessa said. She thought of Tara from her last trip and wondered if she had managed to capture the lake in a painting.

They settled side by side on a flat rock and ate their sandwiches in the sun.

"Look," Ryan said, his mouth full of gooey peanut butter.

Jessa looked where he was pointing. An osprey glided over the water, its wings motionless, braced against the breeze.

"I wish I could fly," Ryan commented.

"Oh, look!"

Jessa held her breath and stopped chewing as the big bird plummeted towards the water. Feet first, it broke the surface, nearly disappearing with a great shimmering splash. Then, with strong downward sweeps of its great wings, the osprey rose up, a glistening fish clutched in its talons.

Still holding the wriggling fish, it flew above the water, a trail of sparkling water droplets falling away behind. It flew quickly away to the far side of the lake and disappeared from sight.

His sandwich still halfway to his mouth, Ryan said quietly, "I've got to go and tell my dad." He scrambled to his feet and scurried back towards camp. Jessa kept staring across the turquoise water towards the point where the magnificent bird had disappeared.

The sun was high in the sky, warm against her cheeks. She closed her eyes and replayed the vision of the bird swooping down from the heavens to capture his lunch. For the first time in weeks, a feeling of complete peacefulness flooded through her.

She opened her eyes and bit into the crisp apple of her lunch. Juice sprayed everywhere and she wiped her chin with the back of her hand. *Jasmine loved apple cores,* she thought.

The idea of riding Jasmine no longer filled her with dread. Being in the mountains was fantastic, but she would be glad to be back home again, riding Jasmine over bigger and bigger fences. A warm breeze touched her cheeks and she closed her eyes again. It wouldn't be long before she and her new mount would be soaring over fences, galloping across open fields, plunging over banks in cross-country courses, and stepping lightly through dressage tests.

Jessa leaned back on her elbows and thoughtfully chewed her apple. She studied the lines of the mountain flanks where they overlapped and folded themselves into the far edge of the glacier-fed lake.

High above her another bird circled—an eagle this time. A little farther along the lakeshore, brown shapes scampered from rock to rock, occasionally standing up to give her a long, inquiring look. The funny creatures were hoary marmots, guardians of the high alpine lakes.

Jessa drew in a deep breath, sucking in the clear,

warm mountain air. She would remember every detail of this day, this afternoon, this moment for the rest of her life. Earlier in the summer it had seemed impossible to think she would ever make it back to Skoki Lake. And yet, here she was, as happy as she could ever remember being.

She heard laughter and talking from somewhere behind her as the others explored the camp and enjoyed their lunch. She took a final bite of her apple and drank in the scene before her, searing every last detail into her memory. Then she got to her feet, had a long, lazy stretch, and made her way back towards where the horses were tethered. Ten to one Spirit would enjoy the apple core as much as Jessa had enjoyed the apple.

Five more days of this, she marvelled. *How lucky could a girl get?*

Author's Note

More than 1.5 million Canadians are affected by diabetes. Approximately 10% have type 1 (or juvenile) diabetes. Diabetes is a leading cause of death by disease in this country.

Though daily insulin injections help people with diabetes control their symptoms, insulin is not a cure. People with diabetes are at higher risk for many serious health complications including vision impairment or blindness, kidney damage, and cardiovascular disease.

My daughter, Danielle, was diagnosed with diabetes when she was six years old. Since then, she has had approximately 10,220 finger pokes, 7,665 insulin injections, 12 hospital stays due to diabetes-related problems, and 728 offers of chocolate bars she had to refuse.

Just because she has diabetes doesn't mean Danielle sits around and mopes! She plays right striker on her school soccer team; rides horses several times a week; plays tennis, volleyball, and squash; and has been a member of her school track team for five years. Since being diagnosed, she has hiked in the mountains of Japan, rollerbladed through Hyde Park in London, and sailed a catamaran in the Bahamas. Danielle's courage, enthusiasm, and love for life provided the inspiration for *Return to Skoki Lake*.

Note that although Jessa is hospitalized for ten days (as was common practice when Danielle was diagnosed), the more typical length of a hospital stay is now just three to four days. Additional diabetes education is then provided through outpatient clinics.

—Nikki Tate

About the Author

The author of seven published novels for children, Nikki Tate has toured schools as a reader and lecturer in four Canadian provinces. She has just returned from a three-week tour of Ontario schools, where she read from her books and explained to the children how she creates stories and how these stories go through many steps before becoming a finished book. She is currently writing her eighth novel for children, as well as a novel for adults.

Tate lives in the countryside of southern Vancouver Island, British Columbia, and goes horseback riding regularly with her daughter, Dani.

Read all the books in the bestselling StableMates Series!

StableMates 1: Rebel of Dark Creek—Meet Jessa, a grade six girl from Vancouver Island, who falls in love with a pony named Rebel. Jessa must learn to juggle school, barn chores, and friendship in this story of determination and ingenuity.

StableMates 2: Team Trouble at Dark Creek—Two giant draft horses arrive at Dark Creek Stables, and Jessa's pony, Rebel, finds himself out in the cold during the worst blizzard of the century. To complicate matters, Jessa and her best friend, Cheryl, have an argument, and an unexpected visitor almost ruins Jessa's Christmas vacation.

StableMates 3: Jessa Be Nimble, Rebel Be Quick—As an eventing clinic draws closer, Jessa needs to find a way to conquer her fears about water jumps. At school she's assigned to help Midori, a new student from Japan, settle in. Cheryl is no help at all—she's too busy trying to land a juicy part in a play.

StableMates 4: Sienna's Rescue—When four abused and neglected horses are seized by the Kenwood Animal Rescue Society, Jessa convinces Mrs. Bailey that Dark Creek Stables would be a perfect foster farm for one of them, but nobody is prepared for the challenges of Sienna's rehabilitation. Can Jessa and her friends save the young renegade mare from the slaughterhouse?

StableMates 5: Raven's Revenge—When Jessa wins a trip for two to horse camp, she and Cheryl are so excited they can hardly think of anything else. But Camp Singing Waters may not be a blissful getaway. Feuding campers, a lame horse and drafty cabins are bad enough, but should they have listened more carefully to Mrs. Bailey's strange comments about Dr. Rainey's experiments with witchcraft? Or, are the late-night ghost stories around the campfire just fuelling their overactive imaginations?

Also by Nikki Tate
and available from Sono Nis Press

Tarragon Island—Heather Blake can't believe her bad luck when her family moves from Toronto to tiny Tarragon Island on the West Coast. What will she, a budding author, write about on this rock in the middle of nowhere? How is she supposed to live without her friends in the writing group and her favourite bookshop with famous visiting authors? Unfortunately, Heather's mother is too busy getting established as the local veterinarian and her father too obsessed with his new sailboat for either of them to pay much attention to her predicament. But with a writer's creativity, Heather finds herself planning a brilliant escape— just like the Count of Monte Cristo.

Set against the backdrop of British Columbia's scenic Gulf Islands, *Tarragon Island* explores the outer and inner landscapes of a young girl struggling to come to terms with the imperfections of her family and herself.

Mystery on Tarragon Island—Adjusting to her family's move from Toronto to tiny Tarragon Island has been difficult for aspiring writer Heather Blake. Thirteen-year-old Heather joins a creative writing class but instead of making friends and working on her novel about poverty and despair, she becomes embroiled in a real-life crime investigation! Meanwhile, she finds herself in competition with an arrogant mystery writer, and in the throes of puppy love.

Nikki Tate writes with verve, humour, and absolute authenticity of twelve-year-old Heather's life-in-transition. Nothing stays the same as Heather's understanding of her island world widens and deepens. Insightful, gentle, a pleasure to read, and wise in its portrayal of Heather's determination to become a writer.
—Marilyn Bowering